Who Buried Sarah?
Eden Monroe

Print ISBNs
Amazon Print 9780228627180
Ingram Spark 9780228627197
Barnes & Noble 9780228627203

BWL Publishing Inc.

Books we love to write ...
Authors around the world.

http://bwlpublishing.ca

I0591948

Dedication

To my good friend, Kay.

Table of Contents

Chapter One

Maude Estey stared disbelievingly at the words written in dark blue ink on pristine white paper. Clutching the note, she began to tremble as she looked around her daughter's bedroom.

ABOUT EIGHT MONTHS EARLIER:

Sarah beamed up at her fiancé as he stood gripping the long-stemmed crystal goblet, his boyishly handsome face alight. "I'd like to propose a toast to the woman I love, the beautiful, the incomparable Sarah Estey who in a few short months will be my wife." He gazed lovingly at her upturned face. "I am a happy man that she has agreed to have me as her husband. I will be even more delighted when she walks down the aisle as my bride. Please stand and raise a toast to Sarah."

He lifted his glass, the icy pink Prohibition mystery punch glittering in the light of the tapered candle centrepiece.

The dinner guests rose as requested, their glasses high, repeating after Connor: "To Sarah!"

Sarah smiled easily, her eyes dancing. She knew every young woman in her set was practically green with envy. That included her best friend, Fanny Hobson, seated across the table from her tonight. After all, Sarah had managed to catch the eye of two of the area's most eligible bachelors. Brothers Dalton and Connor were the sons of prominent Rothesay businessman Pritchard McLagen. First there was Dalton, the inveterate charmer. He had pressed hard for Sarah's hand, foolishly in love with the exquisite preacher's daughter. But then Sarah had met his younger brother, Connor, while Dalton's guest at a McLagen family gathering. Connor was easily the more handsome of the two and there was no denying the immediate chemistry between them. Dalton, whom she'd never seriously considered as a suitable marriage prospect at any stage of their very brief relationship, did not take her rejection well and certainly not when it meant losing out to his younger brother. Connor was well and truly smitten. He'd asked Sarah's father for his daughter's hand in marriage, but Reverend Cranston Estey had ignored the question, continuing to speak as though he hadn't heard him. Refusing to be put off he proposed to Sarah anyway, just four months after making her acquaintance.

Understandably, Dalton had declined an invitation to tonight's celebration. At twenty-six he was a junior partner with the prestigious law firm of Gilbert and Newbury, the McLagen family solicitors for two generations. Like his father, Dalton was charismatic when it suited him, quick to anger when he felt he'd been crossed and was known to hold a grudge.

More personable by far, twenty-four-year-old Connor was apprenticing in their father's prosperous Saint John firm, McLagen & Son Ltd. Located at busy Market Slip on the harbour waterfront, McLagen's was the largest business of its kind in Eastern Canada. Good fortune awaited when The Canada Temperance Act came into effect in 1878, their fortunes increasing somewhat when Prohibition became law again in New Brunswick during the First World War. Pompous and at times ill mannered, Pritchard McLagen had earned his reputation as a ruthless Prohibition opportunist.

The guests resumed their seats at the conclusion of the toast, whereupon Sarah stood and offered a smiling: "Thank you," in response.

As she was reclaiming her seat, she caught the gaze of Agnes McLagen two chairs away and there was no mistaking the flare of hostility in the older woman's dark gleaming eyes. Pritchard and his social-climbing wife were unhappy about this engagement, their favoured son clearly marrying beneath him. Connor remained steadfast in his choice of fiancé and Mother

9

McLagen was barely able to conceal her displeasure. In fact, she'd recently described her future daughter-in-law as a bold, gold-digging hussy when she knew Sarah was within earshot.

An effusive girl, Sarah was not only dazzlingly beautiful, but infectiously high spirited and headstrong. She knew her own mind and had managed to sidestep all attempts by her overprotective parents to match her with their choice of son-in-law, Thomas Chaffee, a thirty-year-old missionary currently serving in The Belgian Congo. She stole a furtive glance at their pinched faces, her mother looking especially miserable. She was shocked they'd come at all under the circumstances, and she'd been afraid her father would somehow sabotage this important occasion. But surprisingly he hadn't, although it was plain they were determined not to enjoy themselves. Both staunch prohibitionists, they hadn't even pretended to sip the punch during Connor's toast. She was well aware they considered either McLagen brother unsuitable for their daughter. After all, her father was dedicated to the church and her mother was dedicated to her father, and the McLagens, while rich and socially popular, were considered by them to be unsavoury.

Sarah exuded warmth and personality, unlike her father the good reverend. Cranston Estey had his nerve passing judgment on others, she thought bitterly.

The man his congregants knew was a far cry from the autocratic tyrant who ruled the Estey household. Her mother, although she loved her dearly, usually went along with whatever her husband dictated, no matter how unfair. Like Pritchard McLagen, Cranston Estey was not to be crossed, although *his* anger was cloaked in righteous indignation. Why, only two nights ago, she'd heard him say when he thought she wasn't listening that he'd rather see his daughter in her grave than tangled up with that McLagen bunch. That only served to make her more defiant. She was eighteen as of last week, a grown woman now and certainly able to make her own decisions.

It was the McLagens who were giving this elaborate engagement party on behalf of their son because appearances must be maintained despite Connor's inflexibility. The event was being held in the dining room of the prestigious Royal Hotel on King Street, in its stately prime after being rebuilt following the great fire of 1877. That massive conflagration was the worst in Canadian history, claiming upwards of twenty thousand lives and razing a good portion of the port city of Saint John. That included the Royal Hotel located on Prince William Street at the time of the fire. The city had risen from the ashes in defiant splendour, with many architectural masterpieces erected in the years that followed.

The Hotel was a gracious host. Following the toast, delicious pineapple upside down cake was served for dessert, still the dessert of choice in 1926. Guests chatted over coffee until Pritchard McLagen brought the dinner to a close in his usual forthright manner.

"Now, everyone, we've had our celebration," he boomed, pushing his considerable bulk to a standing position, "and I thank you for being here with us. Good evening to you all."

Taking the broad hint there was a corresponding scraping of chairs on the polished parquet floor as guests rose obediently to their feet. Ladies' wraps were subsequently fetched, and gentlemen's headgear retrieved. The majority of those present were friends and business associates of the McLagens and appropriately fawning. They were still in high spirits as they made their way out of the hotel and spilled onto the sidewalk. Many opted for a stroll in King's Square, Saint John's garden spot just a short distance up the hill at the top of King Street. The Square was at its loveliest on this unusually balmy late September evening, its abundance of formal gardens still resplendent in their showy summer colours, pigeons billing and cooing at the pedestrians' feet. The City Cornet Band struck up yet another lively tune on the upper deck of the two-story bandstand that straddled the silver dance of the Square's central fountain. The bandstand with its filigree metal framework and copper roof topped with a cornet, had been a gift to the city from the band itself in 1909 as a tribute to King Edward VII.

Connor slid his arm around Sarah's waist possessively as they crossed the street and made their way into the park, Fanny a short distance behind chatting with other guests.

"Connor," Sarah whispered looking up at him, "let's not forget about Fanny. She should be walking up here with us. She is my maid of honour after all."

She glanced back at her best friend, waving her forward. Fanny was easily a head taller than she was and somewhat plain although not completely unattractive. "Come and listen to the band with Connor and me, Fan. What do you say?"

Fanny quickly moved up beside them, looping her arm through Connor's. "I say yes! I'd love to do that. It's such a beautiful night. We won't have many more evenings like this, will we?"

Sarah could read Connor like a book, the slight narrowing of his eyes and the barely perceptible flare of his nostrils. Apparently, he'd wanted this time alone with his fiancé without her friend constantly tagging along, but she felt sorry that Fanny was alone. It was only another hour or so anyway before they started for home she reasoned to herself, and Fanny was right. It was an absolutely splendid evening. Why not enjoy it together?

Connor's cheerfulness sounded forced. "Certainly, by all means join us, Fanny. Let's see if we can find a seat." He paused to assess the crowded square. "I'm afraid we may have to stand. It looks as though all the benches are full."

If Fanny noticed his less than enthusiastic response, it didn't appear to register. That was Fanny for you, thought Sarah. Nothing seemed to bother her. A popular member of the young Rothesay set, she was always up for a lark.

Fanny lived with her Uncle Frederick and Aunt Harriet, her own parents lost during the Spanish flu pandemic that swept with deadly force into New Brunswick in 1918. Fanny had been the only member of her immediate family to survive, so her aunt and uncle had taken her in at the age of ten. Working class people, the Hobsons managed the Dunphy Estate in Rothesay and made their home in a small cottage on the spacious grounds. That meant young Fanny attended school with the sons and daughters of Rothesay's elite, and although poor by comparison she didn't seem to care a whit about that circumstance. Not surprisingly though, she'd chosen Sarah as her best friend. Sarah's own position in life was equally humble, living with her parents as she did in a modest parsonage. Fanny and Sarah might not have been as privileged as their peers, but both girls fit in with the affluent Rothesay crowd.

And then it had been off to Normal School in Fredericton for the two young women where they earned their teaching credentials. Upon completion of their course both were fortunate enough to secure positions at the local school.

"Oh! I see a place to sit," announced Connor suddenly, steering his party quickly toward a tree-shaded wooden bench on the other side of the bandstand. With just enough room for three they settled in as the band launched into another up-tempo selection much to the delight of their audience.

Fanny was practically vibrating with energy. "I feel like dancing," she declared, already moving her feet to the music. "Let's shock these people, Sarah! Let's do the Charleston right here in front of everyone and show them how to have a good time."

Connor caught both of them in his penetrating gaze. "That piece is a march, ladies. It's not a jazz tune so the Charleston would be entirely inappropriate."

Fanny stared at him in surprise as she adjusted her brimless, white cloche hat. It was more for something to do than because it needed adjusting, then began to fidget with the long strand of beads looped around her neck.

Sarah turned to face her fiancé. "Connor, we're just having fun and anyway, I do believe we could dance to that even if it isn't jazz."

Fanny was smiling broadly again. "You know I'd dare to do it, and so would you, Sarah Estey. Come on, it'd be the cat's pyjamas!"

Connor held up his hand in a no-nonsense gesture. "Neither one of you is going to make a spectacle of yourself. Please act like ladies and remember, if you will, that you're both teachers. What would the parents of your students think if they were to see you behaving like that in public? I like to have fun too, but this isn't the time or place to act silly," he continued in undertones. "So sit back and enjoy the music while you can because I want to head for home soon. It's already starting to cool off and I see there's fog gathering out in the harbour."

Fanny flounced back in her seat, although she did so with a good-natured grin as she took her chastisement in stride. "Don't worry, Connor, Sarah and I are not going to embarrass you."

Sarah's eyes twinkled. "I do feel like dancing," she said conspiratorially, "but I suppose we should behave like proper young ladies and maintain a professional decorum."

Connor was still chilly albeit obviously relieved. "Thank you."

Fanny was suddenly serious, as though it had finally sunk in that Connor was perturbed. "Sorry, Connor," she apologized.

"You're right. We were acting like schoolgirls." She returned her attention to Sarah. "It's fun just listening to the band, Sarah, instead of all this talk about dancing. What a silly idea anyway. Say, Connor, what's the name of the tune they're playing now?"

Connor studied the band for a moment before answering, his expression softening. "It's a Sousa march and I must say they're doing a fine job of it. Not much wonder that brass band is so well liked. They always attract a crowd wherever they play."

Fanny nodded. "I agree, they are very good and look at their instruments. Look at how they gleam!"

Sarah, her smile stiffening slightly, swallowed a flash of irritation. That was something that rubbed her the wrong way about Fanny, these days at least. Whenever her best friend spent any time with herself and Connor, Fanny always managed to side with Connor if there happened to be any difference of opinion. It wasn't that she begrudged the attention Fanny showed her fiancé, but just once she could back *her* up. She knew Connor was being polite and patient given the fact Fanny was with them a good deal of the time, so it could be that Fanny picked up on that and was only trying to stay in his good graces. She shook off the small annoyance with an effort, aware that Connor had spoken to her. She looked up at him through wide, cornflower blue eyes that anyone would agree were her best feature. They offset her platinum blonde hair to perfection.

He winked at her. "I caught you daydreaming, didn't I?" he teased. "I said I'll go and get my car and meet you and Fanny on the other side of the Square. I don't want to wait until the fog rolls in before we set off for the country, after all it's at least ten miles to Rothesay."

Within minutes Connor rolled to a stop on the north side of the park in his Ford Model T Roadster, making do with this older car until his new Model A sports coupe was delivered next year. He held the door for each woman in turn as they climbed into the shiny black car.

Indeed, sea fog, chilly and dense, had begun to envelope Saint John's uptown area as they started on their way. They soon left it behind as they headed for Rothesay, passing through tiny hamlets nestled on the banks of the Kennebecasis River.

Once in Rothesay their first stop was Fanny's house. The night was warm again now that they'd left the fog behind, the scent of an autumn-ripened countryside filling the air. Full darkness had descended, and Fanny's Uncle Frederick was silhouetted by lamplight as he pulled the living room drapery aside to verify the safe arrival of his young niece.

Connor alighted first then opened the car's back door for Fanny. "I'll see you in,

Fanny," he said, ever the perfect gentleman as the two headed to the thatched cottage at the end of the cobblestone path.

Sarah watched them walk together. She could not help but appreciate how well-matched they looked walking side by side, but was it always necessary for Fanny to place her arm through his? Fanny appeared to be clinging although it was not generally in her nature to behave that way. Chiding herself, Sarah immediately dismissed the notion of impropriety. Fanny was a dear sweet girl with a pure heart who loved everyone she met and assumed any show of affection was acceptable. She knew Fanny thought of Connor as an older brother, one of the gang. In all fairness she behaved the same with anyone she considered to be a good friend. That was just Fanny's way.

Uncle Frederick opened the door to greet them, and Connor spoke to the big man briefly before quickly retracing his steps to the automobile and sliding behind the wheel.

"Thank you for being so kind to my friend," Sarah told him softly. "Fanny is like my sister. I don't believe I could seriously consider marrying anyone if they didn't regard her as affectionately as I do."

"You know I care about Fanny, darling. I know how important she is to you. Any friend of yours is a friend of mine."

Sarah smiled. She knew he had more to say, so best to let him get it said, "The only problem is ...." she prompted him as he slipped the car into gear and backed down the long, gravelled drive and out onto the road.

Connor sighed deeply as though he was relieved to finally be able to expel it. "All right, the only problem is that sometimes there's too much of Fanny. I would've liked to have you all to myself tonight in the park. I didn't see you inviting your bridesmaids to walk with us. They had sense enough to keep their own company. Mother and Father would have been very happy to drive Fanny home, so I don't see why you had to ask her to be with *us*."

She couldn't help but giggle. She knew she was the ideal match for Connor, the perfect antidote for his moodiness. He did tend to be much too serious at times and she could always be counted on to help improve his frame of mind. She also loved playing devil's advocate on occasion.

"You wouldn't have kissed me in the park, would you, Connor?" she teased. "All we were doing was listening to music and we don't need to be alone to do that, do we? I mean, there were plenty of other people around. Fanny was just one of them."

He braked sharply as a cat dashed into the roadway but made it safely to the other side. "Can I be faulted for not wanting to share your attention with anyone else? The next thing I know you'll be telling me Fanny is coming away with us on our honeymoon." He glanced in her direction before returning his eyes to the road. "You're going to have to learn where to draw the line with her, Sarah. That goes as well for how you behave sometimes. In a few months you'll be a married woman, my wife, and you can't go skipping about as though you were still in pigtails. There is a certain decorum you must maintain as a McLagen and now is as good a time as any to get used to it."

"Connor, this *is* 1926 for heavens sake! Times have changed or haven't you noticed? I'm sure you've heard about the roaring twenties. People don't mind having fun these days, and they don't care who knows it. We're living in a much different world now."

"Thank you for updating me. Now, would you like to go out to Gondola Point and sit by the river for a few minutes?" he asked more kindly. "It's a full moon tonight."

"I'd like that," she said, relieved at the change of subject, as well as the opportunity to be in his arms.

Her mother and father were still very much in favour of the out-dated practice of chaperoning, constantly reminding her that her reputation was at stake going around with Connor as she did. Little did they know.

Maybe a chaperone would come in handy from time to time she thought wickedly, because Connor excited her. He was so handsome with that black hair of his falling rakishly onto his forehead, and those smouldering grey eyes! Just being near him made her heart race. However, outside of a few chaste kisses nothing had happened between them no matter how much her mother wrung her hands, or her father raged against impropriety. It didn't matter a bit to her what people thought anyway, she would do as she pleased. And tonight, she thought with barely concealed glee, she would test the boundaries of Connor's gentlemanly reserve to see if the fire burned as brightly for him as it did for her. Parking in the moonlight in the intimacy of an automobile sounded deliciously naughty.

Connor, unaware of his fiancé's train of thought, pulled in adjacent to the river ferry landing and turned off the motor. The cable ferry was shut down for the night and parked on the other side of the river at Kingston Peninsula ready for its morning traffic.

He slipped an arm around her shoulders. "Sarah, I'm sorry if I was brusque with you. I certainly don't want this celebration to be spoiled by something as silly as a disagreement over whom we share our special night with. I love you, darling. Can you blame me for wanting you all to myself?"

She edged closer, bringing her face to within inches of his and enjoying his spicy masculine scent. "I love to be alone with you, too, Connor. Maybe I'm just a little more patient than you are, at least about that. But here we are now, just the two of us and you have me all to yourself."

His lips found hers with typical restraint. It was more of a brushing of the lips than the passionate kiss she was longing for and determined to make happen.

The thought of Connor turning into a lustful beast amused her. No, he would never be like that, Dalton maybe, but not Connor. Still, she'd like to be surprised. It'd be fun to see what his reaction would be if she pushed him just a little. Let him know she was game for more, should he be so inclined.

She broke off the kiss. Moving closer she sighed provocatively against his ear just long enough to hopefully have the desired effect. She was rewarded with a low groan deep in his throat. Well, it seemed Connor had some life in him after all. Maybe now he'd stop holding back.

She pressed her lips, slightly parted, against his. Connor's hold on her not only tightened but the kiss deepened considerably as he responded hungrily. As it turned out he didn't need much encouragement at all, breathing heavily as they parted.

"What was that all about, Sarah?"

It was a moment before she regained her equilibrium. "It was about me wanting to kiss you, and you wanting to kiss me … properly."

He held her at arm's length. "Properly? I've been doing a poor job of it up 'til now have I? I haven't heard any complaints."

She laughed, although it was a half-hearted attempt. "It's not that you haven't been doing it properly so much as maybe...." she trailed off, suddenly at a loss for words.

"You want me to try to take advantage of you, is that it?"

"Well ... no.... I just thought...."

"Sarah, I want you, but I have respect for you and am prepared to wait for our wedding night. It's only a few months away. Do I have to explain to you the situation we could find ourselves in if we don't wait? I know you're impetuous, but I can't be I'm afraid. I love you, but I'm not willing to subject my family, or yours, to a scandal."

She finally found her voice, embarrassed. "You're right, Connor. I'm not prepared to suffer through something like that either. That would ruin everything. Besides, I know we want to wait awhile even after we're married before we start a family. I only wanted to...."

"Then stop playing with fire. Look, I like it that you want to go further, but not now, darling. We have to wait for the right time, and I promise to live up to your expectations. There will be nothing holding us back then, but I promise I will be gentle."

Shifting away from him slightly, she gazed out across the river. "I understand that. I'm not exactly inexperienced about such things, Connor."

Had she really just said that aloud? She was aghast that the secret she knew she had to share with him at some point had spontaneously bubbled to the surface. This was probably the worst time for such a revelation, but there was no turning back now.

There was silence as she waited for the fallout from the bomb she'd just dropped, not daring to look at him.

"Excuse me?" he asked after a moment, his voice gone hard. "What did you mean by that, Sarah?"

Apparently, this had unexpectedly become the time for truth telling. She was as surprised as he was it was happening, but she loved him too much not to be completely honest. She'd just thought it would somehow be easier to do. "What I mean is ... I've ... ahhh ... been with a man before."

He was deadly calm. "In what way?"

In for a penny in for a pound, so she may as well continue now that she'd started. "In a way that a woman is usually with a man I suppose. You know ... that way."

More silence, in fact it stretched out for so long she wondered if he was going to respond at all. "Do you mean to say you are no longer a virgin?"

She laughed nervously, knowing there was nothing she could say to mitigate the damage. She knew all too well how he felt about such things. "Connor, it was only the once and I...."

Anger sharpened his tone as he began to breathe more rapidly. "You've made love with another man? Is that what you're telling me? That I as your husband will not be the first?"

"I was sixteen and things just got out of hand is all."

"I could certainly see how that would happen given your behaviour here tonight. How old was he, Sarah?" he demanded as though holding onto the hope she had no blame in what had taken place.

"Twenty-five."

"Twenty-five! Was it against your will?"

"No," she whispered. "I knew very well what I was doing, I cannot lie. I was a willing participant, as willing as he was."

Connor swore then, and it was the first time she had ever heard him use profanity. As a matter of fact, she'd never seen her mild-mannered fiancé this angry before. Now that her dreaded confession had been made, the words hung between them ugly and painful.

Wrenching the door open he got out of the car, kicking the front tire angrily before striding away. He stopped beside a tree whose sweeping boughs were adorned with colourful autumn leaves, but she saw no beauty in nature tonight. She just might lose the man she wanted to spend the rest of her life with because of a youthful indiscretion. Times were changing it was true, but she was painfully aware she had violated a sanctity he thought to be inviolable.

She wondered if she should go after him but decided it might be more prudent to wait in the car. Let him get it out of his system. Connor was very levelheaded and probably wouldn't stay angry for long, at least she hoped he wouldn't. The whole thing sounded tawdry without all the details, but she had in fact done what she'd said she'd done without force or coercion. She'd been madly in love with a young man from her church and somehow, they'd managed to escape her parents' watchful eye. Had they been allowed to court in the normal way it might not have come to that stolen moment. Her mother and father had been vehemently opposed because of her age, and *his*, despite the fact he was a member of the good reverend's flock. That was because she'd been promised to Thomas the missionary and it was her rebellious nature that had brought things to a head. The truth was, it had not been an enjoyable experience. She hoped it would be much different with Connor.

The young man had left the area soon after the tryst. She'd pined for him for a while but had eventually recovered and moved on. A year and a half later she'd met the McLagen brothers, Connor quickly stealing her heart. It broke hers to have to tell him he wouldn't be her first, although better now than on their wedding night. It was always better to manage expectations, and he'd certainly know then that she was a woman with a past, as it was considered.

It was close to a half hour before he returned to the vehicle. He shoved himself behind the wheel and slammed the door, his anger having only slightly cooled. When he turned to her, she saw a different man than the laidback Connor she'd made the trip to the Point with. That much was evident, even by the pale light of the moon.

"How many others have there been?" he asked, looking at her coldly. "Is my brother on the list?"

"Connor! Of course not! And besides, I didn't murder someone or rob a bank. I had sexual intercourse, and there was only the one time."

"So you say."

"Yes I do say!"

"Do you love me, Sarah?"

She reached to lay her hand on his arm, but he shook it away. "I asked you a question."

"Yes, I love you, Connor, with all my heart and I want to be your wife. The other was a mistake and it happened a long time ago. I will be a good and faithful wife to you, you'll see."

He sneered. "Right. You lied to me, Sarah. Maybe in a way that's what's most upsetting. I feel betrayed by it all."

"I never lied to you about that. The question never came up."

"You lied by omission! You misled me. You know you did. You know I believed we were saving ourselves for our wedding night. I recall you saying that would make it all the more special, or something to that effect and it wasn't true at all. How can I trust what you say now?"

She dropped her eyes. Guilty. She had played the innocent ingénue, until tonight. "I'm sorry. I know I said that, but I always planned to tell you before then. It never seemed like the right time, and then it just ... came out. I do love you, Connor, and again I'm so sorry. Please believe I love you as much as any woman can love a man."

"I love you too, Sarah, but you've made a fool of me here tonight. I was being so careful with you, so gentle, but it seems you already know the joys of the marital bed don't you?"

She stiffened, outraged. "Connor, that's a terrible thing to say! It's not like that at all. I...."

"Be quiet! As I said you've made a fool of me, but I will not allow that to happen in public, not after our big celebration tonight. There will be a wedding. There would be too many questions asked if we called it off, too much gossip. I'm not prepared to have to deal with that for the sake of my good family name."

"Your good family name!"

He moved his face to within inches of hers although there was no tenderness there now. "Yes, my good family name. The wedding will take place as planned but remember, this changes everything."

Chapter Two

June 1927

"Doesn't your finger get tired carrying that big rock around, Sarah?" teased Fanny during their lunch break at school one day. "How many karats is it anyway?"

Sarah held out her left hand and studied her elaborate engagement ring, then shrugged. "I don't know. I'd never ask Connor such a thing and no, it isn't heavy. He got the fit just right so it's good and snug, otherwise I'd worry about losing it. I'm still very careful when I wash my hands though."

Fanny reached ahead and took hold of Sarah's hand, holding it toward herself at arm's length. "I know I've looked at it before, but I'd forgotten how brilliant those diamonds are. They're especially bright out here in the sunlight. Simply gorgeous! Sarah, I hope you know how lucky you are. Connor is one in a million."

Sarah smiled. "I do know Connor is one in a million. I knew that the first time I saw him. There's no other man for me but him and I'm going to love being his wife."

"And being rich to boot."

"Fanny! That doesn't come into it at all," she scolded her friend playfully. "Mind your manners."

Fanny chuckled, not at all put off. "And he's so nice ... and handsome," she added wistfully. "He's an easy man to love, I guess. I envy you."

* * *

Connor *was* an easy man to love although he was definitely a brooder. He'd yet to say he'd forgiven her for what she'd done, but he'd get past it sooner or later. Sooner would be great, but she just had to be patient.

As her wedding day neared Sarah was busy with fittings, bridal as well as the extensive collection of outfits for her European honeymoon. As a McLagen she'd be expected to be turned out in the latest Paris-inspired fashions, and then there were her maid of honour and bridesmaids' ensembles. She could hardly afford such expense on a teacher's salary, and neither could her parents on a clergyman's budget, so Connor was footing the entire bill. His ardour might have cooled slightly since that dreadful evening at the Point last fall, but he'd stood by his original offer.

* * *

32

Mabel Walker was a dressmaker kept busy by the well-heeled residents of Rothesay and she'd happily accommodated Sarah because the McLagen name carried a great deal of weight in terms of professional goodwill. Connor and Sarah's wedding was to be the highlight of the summer social season, and so she worked around the clock to create an exquisite bridal dress for the petite blonde.

Sarah had fallen in love with the dressmaker's sketches reflecting Sarah's own ideas for something elegant yet modern. Hemlines had begun to rise considerably, and it was now fashionable to show more leg, even at weddings. Gone for the most part were the ostentatious Victorian mounds of lace, ribbons and tulle, and good riddance thought Sarah, wholly in favour of the simpler fare that was now the order of the day.

She was going to Miss Walker's alone today; Fanny and the other girls would be along later in the week. Sarah had lost a few pounds although nothing concerning. It was likely only nerves because her actual wedding to do list was relatively short. It was Connor who was overseeing the army of professionals orchestrating their lavish outdoor wedding reception being held on the grounds of the McLagen estate known as Orchard Hill. There would be plenty of room for the three hundred guests, most of whom were invitees of the McLagens. Sarah's list had been modest by comparison, but she didn't mind. Let them have their furs and finery. She was getting Connor. She could learn to live with the rest.

She covered the short distance to Mabel Walker's house from the school in minutes. The late June air was filled with the fragrance of lilacs, the bushes weighted with the glorious purple blossoms in their final blaze of glory. She was in a pleasant mood as she made her way up the lane to the stately old house the spinster had inherited from her wealthy parents. Miss Walker was known for her crisp astuteness, and Sarah had barely touched her knuckles to the whitewashed door before it was pulled open with purpose.

"Good day, Miss Estey. Come right in, dear, I have your dress ready for the final fitting."

She gave Sarah a meaningful once over. "It doesn't appear that you've lost any more weight, so I think everything is going to be fine. It's not a fitted style as you know, but it does have to hang perfectly. Are you getting excited about your big day?"

Sarah kept pace with the tall woman's generous stride until they found themselves in a large sunlit room filled with fabrics and related paraphernalia. Most important of all there, hanging on the dressmaker's mannequin, was the breathtaking wedding dress of Sarah's dreams transformed into reality.

In keeping with the flapper fashion trend, the dress featured sumptuous layers of ivory silk. The drop waist would give the bride a little more height, and a naughty hemline with tiny pleats allowed for ease of movement. There was also beautiful beadwork and silk embroidery on the slightly capped sleeves. The dress would be accessorized with a matching ornate headband offset by ivory silk T-strap shoes, and despite her love for roses her bouquet would be an enchanting spray of orchids.

She knew she and Connor would look good together, her a vision in ivory silk and he in a black tuxedo with black silk lapels and corresponding black tie. He and his groomsmen would embrace the trend of lighter fabric in salute to the summer season.

Miss Walker slipped the dress over Sarah's slim shoulders, and it whispered into place with the weight of a properly made garment. Once she had been buttoned in the back, she stepped to the full-length trifold mirror and did a slow pirouette, all smiles.

"I love it, Miss Walker! It's absolutely scrumptious and I'm glad you kept the beading and embroidery to a minimum. I don't care for anything that's overdone. It's perfect!"

The seamstress was scrutinizing her work as if daring an errant stitch to reveal itself. She also studied the hemline.

"You're sure that's not just a tad too short, Sarah? You're showing a fair bit of leg, my dear. You don't want to shock people, do you?"

Sarah whirled, loving the caress of the silk against her skin. "I am a thoroughly modern woman, Miss Walker, and this style is all the rage right now. I can't tell you how grateful I am you were able to create exactly what I had in mind. You are a miracle worker. Thank you."

The seamstress coloured slightly, humble despite the fact that her work warranted such enthusiasm. "I'm very glad it suits you, and you do wear it well. I must say I'm very pleased with the result. It's not long now before you'll be wearing it."

"That's right," agreed Sarah, her smile sparkling as she pirouetted yet again, "and I can hardly wait. I'll be Mrs. Connor McLagen in just a few days."

"You're certainly marrying into a prominent family, my dear. I expect you and I will become good friends because I do all of Agnes McLagen's work. I'll likely be dressing you too after you're married. Do you think you'll miss teaching?"

"I will, yes, but even if I were permitted to keep my job, Connor would be dead set against it. As he puts it, there's no room in the workforce for a McLagen wife. It seems I'm to have a very short career in the classroom."

"You'll likely be kept very busy with charity work," said Miss Walker, pushing an errant hairpin back into the substantial bun at the back of her head. "The McLagen's are well known for their philanthropy. But first things first, I also have your trousseau pieces ready along with your travel clothing. I'll arrange to have everything delivered to your home in the next few days."

* * *

Sarah was more than satisfied with Miss Walker's work and it was remarkable how quickly the dressmaker had created an entire wardrobe. She'd never had so many lovely pieces in her life, and that generosity extended to the marital home constructed for them on Maple Lane. She'd been to see it with Connor yesterday and was stunned at how lavishly appointed it was. The house was a gift to them from Pritchard and Agnes. It seemed large for a couple just starting out, but then again, nothing but the best for a McLagen.

But there was a more sobering side to this whole thing and that weighed on her as she headed toward home deep in thought. It was getting used to the fact that other people would again be in charge of her life. Her father-in-law and mother-in-law would pick up where her own parents left off, and she would answer to her husband first. She was determined not to lose herself in the marriage. It was now 1927 after all, and she *was* a modern woman as she had so boldly stated to Mabel Walker just minutes ago.

It was quickly approaching the supper hour as she hurried down the road toward the parsonage where the evening meal was likely waiting to be served. Lost in thought she gave a start when an automobile pulled up beside her. Connor. As always, her heart gave an involuntary lift at the sight of him.

"Get in, Sarah. I assume you're coming from the dressmakers."

"The final fitting," she announced cheerfully. "Oh Connor, you're going to love my dress! I shouldn't tell you too much because it has to be a surprise on our wedding day, but let me just say the hemline is dangerously high." She winked. "It's all the rage!"

He remained unsmiling. "How high?"

"Up to my knees! Isn't that outrageous!"

"I want you in a traditional wedding dress, Sarah, not some contraption that's going to turn you into a laughingstock. I'll speak to my mother who'll speak to Miss Walker. She may have to alter something off the rack, but there's still time to correct this."

"Correct this!"

"Yes, correct this."

"Connor, it's a flapper style. It's the current fashion."

"You are not a flapper! You are going to be a married woman and it's about time you started to act like one. Now get in the car, please."

"I'll walk thanks," she said starting away, her shoulders squared as angry disappointment spiralled through her.

"I said get in the car and stop making a scene."

"*Me* making a scene!"

"Yes, you. People are looking out their windows."

"They're looking out the windows because they don't see many automobiles this far out, that's all. And I got down this road under my own steam and I can get back home the same way. And furthermore, I'm not changing my wedding dress. I told you very well I was going to have the latest fashion, and that's what this is. All you have to do is look at what they're wearing everywhere else. It's in all the newspapers. Besides, Miss Walker agrees with me, and she ought to know. She's a highly respected dressmaker."

He sighed. "Well, I can see I'm outnumbered."

"You are on this one, Connor."

"And I assume it's white."

"Ivory white."

"Of course," he said under his breath.

"Connor," she said, trying to placate him. "Stop this. It's a beautiful dress and I can hardly wait to wear it for you."

He threw up his hands in mock surrender. "Okay, fine. Have your dress. I'm not in the mood to argue. It was a busy day at the office. Now will you please get in the car, dear? I'll drive you the rest of the way home."

She climbed into the passenger seat, and they were soon on their way before she lit the next fuse. "I've decided to get my hair cut into a short bob for the wedding."

He braked suddenly and she was jolted forward, getting her hand onto the dash before she struck it with her shoulder.

"Are you crazy?" she shrieked, relieved that they were now on a stretch of road where there was no one within hearing distance.

"Are *you* crazy?" he yelled back. "You are NOT cutting your hair. I forbid it, Sarah! I like your hair just the way it is."

"It's too long! It would look so much better with my bridal headband if it was bobbed. I might add too that bobbed hair is the latest style. Besides," she said flouncing back into the seat, "it's my hair! I don't tell you how to wear yours."

Connor pulled the car onto the wide tree-lined shoulder. Adjusting himself in the seat he faced her, framing her face with both hands. "Please, Sarah, don't cut your hair. You know how much I like it as it is. That's a picture I've had in my mind ever since I asked you to marry me. Our wedding night, you with your hair unbound, falling over your shoulders. You're so beautiful." He took a loose tendril of hair between his finger and thumb, caressing it. "Your hair is like spun gold. Please, don't take that away from me too. I want you to make that promise."

She looked deep into his eyes, falling into them helplessly. She knew she would give him anything he wanted, except allow any changes to her wedding dress. She smiled tenderly as she brought her hand up and brushed his hair back with the tips of her fingers.

"All right, Connor. I won't cut my hair. I won't say never, but not before the wedding and not unless you feel right about it."

He brushed her lips with a kiss. "I'll never feel right about it, but thank you."

* * *

When he dropped her off at the parsonage, he turned his Model T as quickly as the cramped driveway would allow, and started for home. He hadn't meant to take his sour mood out on his fiancé although she was entirely too cheeky at times. The six years between them sometimes seemed too wide a gap. She was only eighteen after all. He was still put out because of her previous infidelity despite the fact he hadn't known her when it happened. It had been several months now since she'd made that stunning admission. That she'd told him on the night of their engagement celebration, of all times, showed just how immature she really was.

The whole thing still nettled him, but it was rare to find someone of Sarah's beauty and he *was* hopelessly in love with her. He knew he had to let the other go but couldn't see his way clear to let her off the hook ... easily. Not yet. There were parts of the whole thing that would probably never go away, and he worried matters might come to an ugly head on their wedding night when he'd be reminded of just what had been lost.

He next thought of the difficult turn of events at the office today. Damned inspectors! There was always a new face coming along, someone who wanted to make a name for themselves. His father had been apoplectic when that newly minted inspector was able to worm his way in, impersonating an out-of-town client. His father had managed to settle things down, but that meant a costly shipment delay – both coming and going. That's why he was driving down the road this time of the evening, Pritchard had sent him home early and Connor was glad of that because it would give his father time to cool off.

The whole thing could have been hugely embarrassing for the McLagen firm. The majority of the firm's business was legitimate, but they'd also profited substantially on the other side of things over the past several years. While he'd known a bit about local clandestine activity, he'd not realized the extent of his father's involvement.

Things were about to change anyway with the repeal of Prohibition as set out in the Speech from the Throne during the New Brunswick Legislature's spring session. That meant it would soon be legal to purchase alcohol in New Brunswick once again, now at government owned and operated liquor stores, and likely as early as September of this year. Prohibition laws had been nothing but a farce for years anyway he thought, and very lucrative for many. But now legal booze had won the day. Prohibitionists would see this as a disappointing loss, but the truth was there had always been plenty of liquor flowing anyway. The availability of it was the poorest kept secret in town. When someone wanted something to drink it was ridiculously easy to obtain, besides visiting a bootlegger. Just go and see their family druggist for one thing and he'd write a prescription for the stuff. Druggists were the busiest men around come Christmas because there was always a ready supply for a price.

He shook his head. He knew he was much too serious about things, much like his father in that regard he could see. That was the case with this thing with Sarah too, returning to his original concerns. What will it be like to be married to her he'd often asked himself these past few months. The answer as usual came bouncing back at him in a flash. It will be a challenge. She wasn't one to back down and she seemed to delight in hitting him with the unexpected, always pushing at the boundaries. Wouldn't he be in for much more of the same after they were married? Or could he tame her? His one big payoff was that he would get to have sex with her, his first with anyone. But then again someone else had gotten there first on that too, hadn't they? At least he'd have a beautiful wife, one that every other man would be envious of and that pleased him to no end.

He had to go ahead with the wedding. It was too late to change his mind now ... wasn't it? He could picture her, standing before him, naked, her hair a halo of pale gold silk tumbling over her shoulders. But there was a lot more to be considered than the bedroom. He balled his fists. No, today was not a good day. Maybe he should have a nice long talk with her, get a few things straightened out before they said 'I do.' That might be the thing right there. He'd settle her down, lay everything right on the line. It was her free spirit, in addition to her beauty that had attracted him, but now he wondered how easy she'd be to manage. Could love overcome everything?

* * *

Sarah glanced back at Connor before starting inside. Her idea had been to blow him a kiss, but he hadn't even glanced in her direction before his abrupt departure. She shrugged off the rebuff. Connor had been especially difficult lately, but that would all change once they were married and settled down, she told herself. He just had to see for himself what a wonderful wife she would be, how wisely he had chosen. But then there was his darker side.

She heard voices as she stepped into the vestibule, her mother hurrying to meet her. "Come along please, dear. You're late. I've been doing my best to keep the meal warm. Were you delayed leaving school? Is that it?"

Sarah was mildly annoyed. "I told you I'd likely be late because I had to go to Miss Walker's for a fitting today. That's where I was."

Maude Estey looked away. "Oh, yes, that."

Sarah chose to ignore her mother's tone. "Mother, you should see my dress. It's exquisite. I wish you could have come with me to the fitting, but you said you were busy."

"I was busy, dear, preparing our evening meal. Now do hurry, we have a guest and we've kept him waiting long enough."

"Him?" she asked, alarm bells starting to go off in her head.

"Yes, him. He's a dear friend of ours … all of us."

She followed her mother into the dining room where the table was laid for four, her mother's good dishes and best cutlery in place on white linen.

"Who….?" She started to ask her mother, but just then her father and Thomas Chaffee entered the dining room from where they'd been talking in Reverend Estey's study. Her mouth fell open.

Thomas regarded her with a wide grin, his sandy hair cut neatly but his moustache would be considered ragged by anyone with good taste. "Sarah, how wonderful to see you, my dear. I've been counting the minutes until we meet again."

Sarah stared.

Maude Estey was fluttering about like a nervous bird. "Let's all sit, shall we? I've made a lovely stew for our supper, and it will be off its best if it stands much longer."

They all sat down, and Sarah was at least glad the seating arrangement meant she would be across from Thomas, rather than beside him.

Maude set a large ceramic soup tureen in the centre of the table, and each ladled a generous portion into their bowls, except for Sarah.

Once grace had been said Thomas dove in to start the conversation rolling again. "I say, Sarah, you look even more beautiful than when I saw you last time, if that's possible."

Sarah's stomach had turned on her in full mutiny. Eating was out of the question at the moment although she went about the pretence of doing so. "Thank you," she mumbled. "You're looking well too," she thought to add out of common courtesy.

Reverend Estey buttered a warm roll with gusto. "Thomas is home on furlough," he said, directing his remarks to his daughter. "He was just telling me all about his wonderful missionary work in The Belgian Congo. Say, son, tell Sarah about that narrow miss you had with the herd of elephants."

Thomas swallowed what he had in his mouth before setting off on his story. "It happened about a month or so ago, I guess. The children had just finished for the day in our little school when a whole herd of elephants came stampeding through our village. There must have been ten or twelve of the huge beasts in all. We're not sure what spooked them, but their trumpeting was terribly loud, and they were kicking up so much dust we could hardly see."

Sarah feigned interest only because it was polite to do so but did feel empathy for those involved. "That would have been terrifying. Was anyone injured or killed?"

Thomas smiled at her, clearly besotted. "Everyone was able to get out of their path although there was a lot of damage done. Some of the huts were completely demolished as you can imagine. For a few minutes I thought surely the little school would also be flattened, but it was spared. Thank God. It all ended as quickly as it began, I'm happy to say, but that's what one can expect when one is in the wilds of Africa. Having said that I can't imagine doing anything else with my life. I'll never be sorry I went there. But that was an isolated incident," he hurried to explain. "Life there is tranquil in the extreme."

Sarah nodded, a smile frozen solidly in place. Relax she told herself, Thomas was an old friend of the family. If he was home on furlough it would be perfectly understandable to be invited to the home of Reverend Estey, the minister of the church that Thomas served. "You're a very brave man, Thomas," she said, "and I would say you're perfectly suited for the job you're doing."

Thomas was still regarding her with lovesick calf eyes set in a small head on a long neck. "It's not a job, Sarah. It's a calling."

Sarah nodded. "Perfectly suited to your calling then," she quickly amended.

Her father was not to be left out of the conversation for long. "Sarah's a teacher now, Thomas." He turned his attention to his daughter. "Sarah, tell Thomas about your work in the classroom."

Sarah was still toying with her stew. "There's not much to tell really. I adore children. This year I taught first and second grades. Naturally it was a challenge to get the little ones settled in and now the school term is nearly over. The time has flown."

Thomas swallowed another mouthful. "It sounds fascinating."

Sarah had an idea he'd say the same thing if she'd just announced her job was watching paint dry. "I'm sure you understand from your own experience as a teacher, there's no end of surprises when it comes to children."

A voracious eater, her father had very nearly cleaned his bowl, mopping up what was left with the remnant of a roll. "Thomas was telling me they need teachers in the village where he's working."

Sarah knew the direction her father was attempting to steer the conversation. "I can't imagine you'd have many students. Didn't you say it was a very small village?" she asked Thomas.

The missionary nodded over-eagerly. "It is a small village, but we have twenty-two students of various ages, from six to fifteen, so you can understand how challenging it would be to meet all of their needs. That includes Bible study, which is at the forefront of our curriculum. Ethel Sparks has just retired and her shoes are going to be hard to fill. Help is always needed."

Sarah did manage to get a scant spoonful of the stew down. "I'm sure there are always plenty of missionaries available to fill those vacancies."

Reverend Estey was not known as a man to beat around the bush, and he didn't now as he nudged his empty bowl aside. "Sarah, you would be perfect to fill that role. There would be some additional training required and Thomas would be there to help guide you through the process. Just think of the adventure too, you would be experiencing life on the Dark Continent. I've heard that once you go there you never want to come back, it's that beautiful."

Thomas had also polished off his helping of stew. "Amen to that, Reverend Estey. I can think of no happier life. The only thing that would make it better would be to share it with someone very special."

Sarah almost dropped her spoon. If she didn't know any better, she'd say she was on a runaway train, one that was going to zoom past the station on its way to who knows where.

Maude Estey dared to speak, as though forgetting her mealtime input was not required. That was one of Reverend Estey's unspoken rules. His observations and opinions were the only ones that counted, never his wife's.

"I say, Sarah, are you feeling all right?" Maude asked. "You've just gone very pale."

Reverend Estey reprimanded his wife with a glare. "It's her colouring, Maude. There's no need to become flustered. Now, let's get to the meat of the matter. Sarah, Thomas has asked for your hand in marriage, and I have very happily given both my consent *and* my blessing."

Chapter Three

Connor was still deep in thought as he made his way home after dropping Sarah off. Should he be this troubled about the wedding with it just days away? He loved her but was it enough?. True, money had been spent, invitations sent, all the wedding apparel, for both sides, had been created, the caterer making last-minute arrangements ... and the list went on. Could it all be stopped now without calamitous results? Did he want to stop it? It was probably just the proverbial nerves, and they would go away. They had to. After all, where would he find another Sarah? She was so beautiful ....

He was still in a poor mood by the time he arrived home. His mother was in the living room, reading, when he let himself in.

"Hello, darling!" she welcomed him. "You're home very early today. Is everything okay?"

He was not about to go into the brouhaha at the office today. That storm had likely not even begun to subside, and he dreaded when his father arrived home. He'd likely have something more to say to him about inviting that inspector into the inner sanctum, as innocent a mistake as it had been.

"Hello, Mother," he replied, starting for the stairs at the other end of the hall. He needed the quiet of his room to continue sorting out his thoughts.

"Where are you off to so quickly, Connor? Come and sit with me. Your father won't be here for at least another hour and Cook is just beginning to prepare dinner."

He swallowed his irritation. "Mother, I thought I'd go and lie down before dinner. I have a headache."

"Nonsense, you can spare me a few minutes," she told him, indicating the armchair opposite her with a sweep of her hand.

He gave in, settling into the floral damask wingback with a sigh.

"Didn't I see you go by about a half hour ago with that Estey girl in the passenger seat?" she asked him.

He studied his mother. That *Estey girl* was going to be her daughter-in-law in very short order, but neither of his parents had even begun to accept the inevitable. You can't mix classes, was the one constant in all of their many protests. He had exhausted himself trying to bring them around. It was all about financial status in that community, old money, new money, and those with very little of either.

Pritchard, a wealthy McLagen, had married Agnes Stipley of Renforth, daughter of King's Counsel barrister and solicitor, and later Court of King's Bench judge, Matthew Stipley. That's how it was done. Connor had chosen from the wrong side of the tracks.

He worked to keep his tone civil. "I was giving Sarah a drive. I came upon her walking home from the dressmakers."

Agnes laid her book down on the mahogany side table. "I saw her walk by earlier and I assumed that's where she was headed. Most everything is in place for the *wedding* I assume," she said with sarcastic emphasis, as though she was talking about a scheduled execution. He supposed to his mother it was one and the same. "This is all quite a step up for a minister's daughter."

"Mother...."

"All I meant is that she's doing very well for herself. I would imagine Reverend Estey and his wife have been only too glad to welcome you into their lives."

"Right," he snorted with derision. "I've already told you they don't like the McLagens."

Agnes brushed an imaginary fleck of lint from her navy linen dress. "That just goes to show their ignorance. If ever there was a sanctimonious pair, it's them. They don't know when their daughter's well off. She's certainly bettering herself."

Connor dropped his head back against the chair cushion with more force than he intended, punctuating his dour frame of mind. "Can we not talk about this, Mother? I told you I have a headache, and this certainly isn't helping."

Agnes took his measure and backed up slightly. "I intended to tell you as soon as you came in the door, Connor, that Gladys Biddington called for you."

That got his attention, his head coming up sharply. "Gladys called for me? What did she want?"

"I'm assuming she wanted to speak with you. She asked that you give her a call when you came in."

"I don't believe I have anything else to say to her."

"You broke that girl's heart, Connor, without so much as a by your leave. You know she believed you two would marry. Now that's a marriage we all wanted ... still want," she added under her breath as she watched him closely.

"Gladys and I straightened everything out a long time ago."

"Did you?"

"Well certainly, Mother. I met Sarah and...."

"And dropped Gladys," Agnes finished for him, folding her arms. "It was a very cruel thing you did to her. Do you know her parents, James and Kitty, will no longer take our calls? We invited them to our New Year's levy and they were the only ones to decline. You offended some very dear friends, not to mention alienated one of your father's biggest clients. And all because you took up with that Estey girl. In any event, Gladys has called for you and the very least you can do is call her back and see what it is she has to say. She's very gracious, well bred, so she likely only wants to wish you the best."

"I'm not at odds with Gladys." He shrugged. "She understands I fell in love with somebody else. It happens all the time. I certainly didn't invent it."

"I would suggest you speak with her. I told her you would so now you must."

"I must?"

"It would be the proper thing to do. Really, Connor, since you've been keeping company with that Estey girl your manners have flown right out the window. You used to be such a polite boy, not like your brother who says whatever comes into his head."

"Mother, I'm a man, not a boy, and yes, I will contact Gladys. Okay?"

Agnes fixed him with a level stare. "Don't take that tone with me, Connor. Perhaps you'd better go up and lie down for a while after all, and I hope you come down in a better mood."

* * *

Time alone in his room did *not* put him in a better mood and when he heard his father come in an hour or so later, he knew before Pritchard bellowed his name from the bottom of the staircase that he was still angry. It crossed his mind to ignore him, but his more prudent side told him nobody ignored Pritchard McLagen, not for very long. It only made matters worse.

Heaving himself off the bed he made his way slowly to the top of the stairs. "Yes, Father?"

It appeared as though Pritchard was making an effort to stay calm. "I'd like to see you in my study straight away."

Connor did as he asked and soon the two men were seated across from one another behind closed doors. "First of all, I'm sorry, Connor, for raising my voice to you earlier today. I understand it wasn't your fault letting that inspector in. I ought to have been more forthcoming with you about our, situation, shall I say? As you are aware, Prohibition is a taboo subject here in this house because in my opinion it makes for poor dinner conversation. But I'll make an exception for the purpose of *this* conversation. First of all, I don't believe in it. I don't believe the state has a place in the homes of sensible people who ought to know how to run their own lives. If they want a drink, they bloody well should be able to have it."

One thing Connor could say about his father, for all his bluster he did allow his sons to speak their mind. If either he or Dalton had an opinion they wished to express, they were encouraged to do so no matter how vigorously he might disagree with it. His father's pause seemed to encourage that at the moment, so he took full advantage of the privilege.

"Father, I must say I don't understand why you're not in favour of Prohibition. You're a teetotaller, and...."

Pritchard reddened slightly. "Be that as it may, son, I don't feel government has the right to speak for everyone. It is my choice not to drink. I do not care for the stuff, but what kind of world would it be if everyone did exactly as they were told by someone who thought they knew better? Many a fortune has been won or lost on liquor, Connor, boon or bust, but that's all the use I have for it."

Connor could think of a dozen different arguments to counter his father's, like families who suffered because a loved one had the disease of alcoholism. He'd seen that firsthand through a friend of his at school.

How could he tell his father he was contradicting himself? Not supportive of Prohibition yet profiting from it. That his father's company, and some day his, was routinely breaking the law, conveniently positioned as they were on the waterfront in a port city. Pritchard McLagen knew enough to stay far enough back to keep his hands clean inasmuch as he never touched a bottle.

"So because you don't agree with the law it's okay to break the law?"

"When it's a bad law, yes."

"But, Father, that's wrong, isn't it?"

Pritchard held up his hand. "I would suggest you remember yourself, son. I'm in favour of open conversations, but there is still a line not to be crossed and you're dangerously close to doing just that at the moment."

"But if we're breaking a law, doesn't that make us McLagens criminals?"

Pritchard's colour continued to deepen. "No, we are not criminals in the sense you suggest. I am a highly respected businessman who gives back generously to the community. I also provide lavishly for my family, and you are training to follow in my footsteps." He settled back into the chair, the leather squeaking in protest as he adjusted his bulk. "You're young, Connor, but you will see as you go along and learn more that it's necessary at times to bend the rules. That's how business is done, successful business anyway. I can't stand in judgement of every request that comes across my desk. It's supply and demand, son. The United States is dry as dust, much worse than Canada, and if a man wants to enjoy a glass of sherry after his evening meal, what harm is there in that? A glass of wine on a special occasion? You have to look at the big picture."

"But it's whiskey primarily."

Never long on patience, Pritchard's control snapped. "Do not play semantics with me, boy!" he barked. "And do not question my business practices. McLagen &

Son has been in operation for close to a hundred years. We did not succeed by pussyfooting around and worrying about whom we might offend. Any liquor we *export* we do so under the full protection of Canadian law. We have many employees with families to feed and that also has to be taken into consideration. I'm not running a charity. I'm running a business. Do you think this is the first storm we've ever had to weather as a company? Prohibition was put in place to solve any number of social problems, but that's not what everyone wants. If someone doesn't want to drink, don't drink. What right do they have to deprive others of it?"

"What happened to caring about people's health?"

"Open your eyes, young man! I knew Prohibition would eventually be repealed and not because they care a whit about anyone's health. It's because they need the taxes from the sale of alcohol to modernize the province, make important infrastructure changes. They need that revenue to build roads, dams, schools, hospitals. At the end of every discussion is money, the almighty dollar, and we're no different. A man does what he has to do to stay afloat and don't you ever forget that. This company will be yours someday, Connor, and by the time you're through your apprenticeship with me, I guarantee you'll be ready to run it the way it's supposed to be run. It's wonderful to have ideals, it's much more difficult to live up to them."

"But what about drunkenness? What alcohol does to families? Wasn't that the original argument for Prohibition?"

"What about it? Look, Connor, it's a societal ill. I can take you to any number of places right this minute and show you someone who's drunk. And you know what the difference is? If they were drunk without Prohibition, the government would have made enough off the bottle in taxes that they should probably leave them alone. If they find that person drunk *during* Prohibition, they'll make money from fining them, but not as much as they'd have made from taxes. The government will always get its money one way or another. Hell, people wanting drink contributes to a great extent to the financial stability of this province, the tax revenue from it."

"I still wonder about the whole thing. Making sure you get a bottle into peoples' hands."

Pritchard eyed him without speaking for a few moments. "It's that Estey girl, isn't it and her moral high ground? They're all a bunch of do-gooders. She's got you thinking like this."

"Sarah's got nothing to do with any of this."

"I'll say one thing, if she ever comes snooping around my business, she'll be very sorry and you can tell her that for me. Her or any of her people."

"I told you, it's not Sarah. I have my own moral compass." Connor paused for a moment, considering the sound aspects of his father's point. People, and businesses in particular, *were* overtaxed. Maybe it was their right to level the playing field. Still.... "I hear you, Father, but I have my own mind in these things."

"And now you've spoken it, and I've spoken mine, but you are to in no way repeat what you and I or anyone else discusses at McLagen & Son with outsiders, including your wife. I warn you, Connor, leave this alone. I decide the type of business my company does at the present time, you just work there. You are not to question my decisions. Am I making myself clear about that?"

"Yes, sir."

"When you're running the business someday you will be making all company decisions, until then it's mine and I will run it as I see fit whether you agree or not. Again, do you understand what I'm saying to you?"

"Yes, Father, I do. And don't worry, I'll keep this discussion and any others like it, to myself."

"There will be no further discussions on this subject other than perhaps something you're not sure about. In that case you're to come directly to me. That includes anyone sniffing around, asking questions. What happened today will not happen again."

"I'm very sorry about that. I thought that guy was a friend, a client."

"Certainly not a client, although he was clever about it, and definitely not a friend. He was an adversary, but I have dealt with it and that's the end of it."

"What about Mother?"

Pritchard looked genuinely perplexed. "What about her?"

"I mean as far as the business is concerned. Does she share your views?"

"Connor, my boy, you do have a lot to learn. Your mother is not involved in any way shape or form with McLagen & Son Ltd. She has no interest in such things. Her only connection is that she enjoys spending the money the company earns, and I enjoy providing her with the luxuries she is accustomed to."

"But if she knew...."

Pritchard's face darkened again. "She would feel the same way I do, but that's neither here nor there. Your mother may not have a mind for business, but she is a very astute woman, and I would trust her opinions ... and loyalty in all things. But how I conduct my business is my concern and nobody else's. Now, I thank you for your point of view. I feel we've both been given an opportunity to be frank with one another and this is where it stops."

"Again, sir, I understand."

"Fine, now I understand dinner is about to go on the table and Lavinia does not like us to be late. Let's head for the dining room. Besides, now that the air has been cleared, I'm starving."

Once the evening meal was finished Connor excused himself from coffee and dessert, instead heading to his room where he freshened up and changed his clothes.

He looked at the piece of paper where his mother had noted Gladys' telephone number. He could call her but decided to pay her a visit instead. He wasn't necessarily in favour of telephones anyway. They were a wonderful convenience at work, but far too impersonal otherwise. Besides, Gladdy, as all her friends called her, must have something important to say to him if she'd made that call in the first place. She'd understand too, it could have been accomplished over the telephone without half the community listening in because his family had a private line installed. Still, he wanted to see her.

It was an idyllic June evening as he climbed into his automobile and started for the Biddington's mock Tudor home where he and Gladys had so many lively times while they were dating. He'd thought he loved Gladys and had even hinted there might be a future for them one day. That was before Sarah had swept him off his feet. The fact that he'd been able to take her away from Dalton was an impressive personal accomplishment, and she belonged to him now. What man wouldn't want Sarah Estey on their arm? She was a trophy for sure, whereas Gladys was only passably pretty although steady as a rock and thoroughly likeable. Compared to Sarah she was boring, or was that what a man needed in the long run?

Gladys answered the door on his first knock, and he was struck by the change in her appearance since he'd last seen her. She was much slimmer, and she'd bobbed her hair which was most becoming, accentuating her large dark eyes. Her smile was more fetching than he remembered, her lips soft and full.

"Connor, I'm surprised you came here," she said. "I just thought you'd call. I'm so excited that Daddy finally gave in and got a telephone so I'm happy to have a chance to use it. He said he never would because he's kind of set in his ways, so Mother and I were very glad when he changed his mind."

"I could have called, but I needed to get out of the house for a little while and breathe some fresh air. So here I am. How have you been?"

She stood back from the door. "Come in, Connor. There's no need to stand on the doorstep. I'm all alone tonight anyway because Mother and Daddy are at dinner over at the Mallards."

Connor hadn't been at the Biddingtons for well over a year, and it felt good to be back in this comfortable old house. He liked Gladdy's mother and father. They'd always been kind to him, and he'd eaten many meals here during the three years he and Gladys had been together. That good relationship had gone south when they'd broken up. Gladys had taken it hard, as had her parents.

He followed her into the large living room where he settled onto a corner of the sofa. She sat across the room in an overstuffed armchair.

"So, Gladdy, what's on your mind? Why did you call me?"

She blushed. "You'll probably think me a silly goose, but I wanted to talk to you, Connor. I was going to ask you to come over so we could speak in person, but I didn't know if you'd come or not."

He smiled. "It seems I've read your mind because here I am. Now that I am here, what did you want to talk to me about?"

She seemed suddenly nervous. "About us," she said, holding his gaze. "You broke my heart when you told me we were through, Connor. It still hurts as much now as it did that night. But a long time has passed, and I thought maybe...."

He nodded with chagrin. "You're right. It was a terrible night, and I could have done a much better job of ending things between us. I didn't want to hurt you, Glad. I thought a lot of you, I still do, and we did have some wonderful times together. It just didn't work out in the long run is all."

She studied him for a moment before she spoke. "And you've never had any second thoughts about it? I wanted to call you so many times, but I thought no. Let him have time to reflect, to think, and he'll see what we had together was too good to let go. You met this new girl and within months you were engaged. Things just seemed to go so fast. I couldn't believe it when I heard you were getting married. I mean so soon."

He shifted uncomfortably. Did she have to look at him that way? Those big sad puppy dog eyes had always gotten to him.

"It's true, Gladdy, I am getting married. Everything is set. It's going to happen in just a few days."

Tears sprang to her eyes. "So it's actually true?"

"Yes, it's true. We had a big engagement party last September in Saint John, so it's been official for a while now."

Her tears were dangerously close to falling. "But it's not fair, Connor. She will never be as good for you as I am. We both know that. I understand she's very young."

"Not that young, she's eighteen. I'm only six years older than she is."

She dabbed at her eyes with a lace-edged handkerchief. "She's still a teenager, Connor, whereas I am the same age as you. We both want the same things, we always have. You can't have forgotten that. You told me you never felt so comfortable as when you were with me, more able to be yourself. I waited for you while you were away at university. Remember? I was faithful to you. I've never been with anyone else. There's only ever been you, and that's still true."

Those words struck a nerve and he hoped she hadn't noticed. Faithfulness was a very important thing in a relationship, trust. That was still a sore spot where Sarah was concerned although she had not given him any other reason to doubt her. It still stung that some other man had taken her virginity, and not him.

"And I was faithful to you when we were together, Gladdy. I never looked at anyone else either."

"You and I both know that's not true," she said quietly, her eyes still bright with unshed tears. "You not only looked at the first person who came along, you dropped me for her. I never even knew you'd met another girl until I heard it from Jenny Plascoe."

He nodded, knowing he deserved everything she said. "I know I put it off too long because I was dreading letting you down. For that I apologize from the bottom of my heart. I want you to be happy, Glad, I really do. You are a wonderful person and I want you to meet someone who will love you and stay by your side forever. I'm not that person anymore. I was at one time but not now. I'm sorry."

A tear slipped down one cheek and then the other. "So, I've lost you all over again," she whispered with emotion.

"Gladys...."

It was a few moments before she regained her composure. "Tell me, Connor, honestly, are you going into this marriage with any doubts?"

"Well, I...."

"I'm being your friend right now when I say this, Connor. If you have any doubts whatsoever about this, don't marry her."

Chapter Four

Sarah gaped at her father. She had never openly defied him before, but her blood rose to the surface like heat lightning. "Thomas has asked for my hand in marriage, and you have given your consent? Your blessing? I do believe I'm in the middle of a nightmare." She held up her ring finger. "Father, I am engaged to another man. Connor McLagen and I are going to be married. My hand is not available to anyone else for the asking. It's taken."

Reverend Estey's face shot from pink to purple in nanoseconds. "You are not married yet, Sarah. I forbid you to marry that … criminal!"

Sarah rose to her feet indignantly. "Criminal! You may not care for Connor or his family, but he is a good and decent man, not a *criminal* as you put it. I will soon be Mrs. Connor McLagen and there is nothing you can do about it, Father!"

Reverend Estey had also gained his feet. "I have gone along with this whole charade for as long as I intend to. I have made my feelings known to you, child, but you continue to defy me." He pointed to her diamond ring. "The very ring you're wearing is cursed with crooked money. That is not how you were brought up, to consort with thieves."

Maude Estey laid her hand on her husband's arm in an attempt to placate him. "Now Cranston, there's nothing to be gained by a shouting match. Perhaps if we all sat down and spoke calmly and reasonably, we could resolve this."

Reverend Estey shook his wife's hand away impatiently. "Be quiet, Maude! Are you completely dense? You are interfering in a matter being dealt with by the head of the household. She is still my responsibility, and I will not stand by, even at this eleventh hour and watch her make such a terrible mistake."

Maude had begun to wring her hands. "Cranston, I do believe...."

Reverend Estey's eyes were on fire as he turned his full attention on his wife. "I said shut up, Maude! You have nothing worthwhile to contribute. Now I told you to go about your business and let us be. Go!"

Maude wrenched herself away from the table and hurried from the room in tears, one hand to her mouth.

Thomas got to his feet, his arms folded. "Sarah, my darling, why won't you listen to reason? I don't know the man you say you're going to marry, but I *can* say with certainty he'll never be as good for you as I will be. I am one hundred percent in agreement with your father. You are headed down a ruinous path. You can't marry someone like him when you belong in the mission field with me. We will work together, that's always been my dream."

She spun on him. "*Your* dream! Not my dream! I wouldn't marry you if you were the last man on earth! I have nothing bad to say about you, Thomas, only that I don't love you. I would be miserable married to you."

Thomas's hands were now on his hips. "I am a good man! Can you say the same about this Connor character?"

Sarah was incredulous. "Of course I can. Just because he's not doing the same thing you are doesn't mean he's not good too. Connor is a wonderful man, and he wants only the best for me. How can you condemn someone you've never even met?"

Any attempt at a smile had vanished from Thomas's face. "Because your father, whose opinion I trust above all others, has told me all I need to know. He knows the family and they're wicked, not to be trusted. The thought of you marrying into that makes me sick to my stomach."

Sarah threw caution completely to the wind. "You're not marrying him, neither of you are," she said swinging her head in her father's direction before returning her attention to Thomas. "I'm the one who is marrying him, and I couldn't be happier. I am eighteen years old! I am a full-grown woman and I know what I want."

Her father pounded the table with a fist. "You are nothing but an addlebrained girl who for some unearthly reason finds great pleasure in defying me. You have acted out before, but this time you're going much too far. You will not marry that man!"

Sarah's voice had climbed several octaves. "I will marry that man and make no mistake about it. Why do you have to try to make my life so impossible? I'm going to be a married woman and what I do with my life from that point forward will be between my husband and me. Now if you'll excuse me, I've suddenly lost my appetite."

With that she left the table and headed for the back door, her father's: "Sarah! Come back here when I'm talking to you!" booming in the background. The last thing she heard before she left was: "Thomas, go after her and talk some sense into her."

She hoped the neighbours hadn't heard the shouting match. They probably hadn't because the parsonage, adjacent to the church, sat off by itself surrounded by a forest of tall lilac bushes. Slipping her arms into the light jacket she'd grabbed from a hook beside the door, she set off for Saint Paul's Anglican Church located as its name suggested, on Church Avenue. There was no activity there tonight, so she'd sit for a while on the front steps as she often did while out for a walk.

"Sarah, wait up!" she heard Thomas call from behind.

She did not slacken her pace. She could hear his shoes slapping gravel as he sprinted to cover the distance between them. If anyone happened to go by and see him chasing her, she'd be mortified, Estey family drama spilling out onto the main road. She stopped and turned, waiting for him to catch up. "Thomas, I want to be alone. Please go back to the house."

He put his hand on her shoulder as he fought to catch his breath. "Sarah, I don't want things to be like this."

"Then leave me alone. I will never marry you, Thomas. I am going to marry Connor McLagen and there is nothing more to discuss."

"You don't understand. Your father and mother want you to marry me. I'm the man they've chosen for you. If you insist on going through with that other wedding, your father will put a stop to it. He'll disrupt the service and he means it."

She struggled to remain calm. "My father is a bully, and you are too if you think you can force me into marrying you."

Perspiration beaded his forehead, his neatly combed hair now askew. "But we're destined to be together. You would love Africa, Sarah."

"I have no doubt that I would love Africa," she said, setting her jaw, "but I will never love *you*."

"Maybe not right now but I'm willing to wait for you. Give this thing some time,

Sarah. You are impetuous, but I beg you to reconsider all of this before it's too late."

"Thomas, listen to me! Hear me! I am not going to marry you, ever, and I don't know how exactly, but I will make my father see reason. He has a short memory. He as good as gave Connor his consent because he wouldn't answer him when he asked to marry me. He likes to forget that, but that's what happened. He didn't say no. Now I'm going for a walk, and I hope you'll be gone when I get back home. Good-bye, Thomas."

"You won't reconsider?"

"No, not ever, and that is my final answer. I can be just as stubborn as all of you. Good-bye."

Thomas at least had the good grace not to press the matter further as she started away again. When she dared peek over her shoulder he was indeed walking slowly back to the parsonage.

The evening had not yet begun to cool as she covered the remaining distance to the church and sat midway up the steps. She needed to clear her head after that fiasco with her father and Thomas Chaffee. How could she make her father understand once and for all she was going to marry Connor McLagen? Nothing was going to change her mind, not at this point. Preoccupied she didn't notice the man approaching her until he'd sat down beside her on the step.

"I thought that was you," he said in a husky voice. "I was driving by and said, my goodness! That's Sarah Estey over there. I parked right away and came to see for myself. How are you doing anyway?"

She groaned inwardly. Of all the people she had no wish to see right now, or any time come to that, it was Dalton McLagen. Nevertheless, here he sat mere inches away.

"I decided to get out for a walk because it's such a lovely evening and this is a nice place to sit and enjoy it."

He looked around as if to verify her description before returning his gaze to her. "I suppose it's okay, but a real chair would be better. I would think you'd get enough of this area during the day though, what with the school so close and all. It hasn't closed yet, has it? School, I mean."

"Not long now before it's let out for the summer. It's hard to keep the children's attention with their holiday so close at hand. They're young and they've had enough of sitting in a classroom all day."

Dalton crossed his legs as he settled back. "Oh, to be young again, a child waiting for summer vacation. We never know when we have it good until it's past. I suppose that's just human nature."

She nodded. "Very true. How is the legal profession treating you these days, Dalton? Are you seeing much of the inside of a courtroom?"

He shrugged. "I've partnered on a couple of substantial cases in the past year, other than that it's just the usual spade work one does as a legal professional. It's not all fireworks. There is a fair amount of plodding involved."

"You're not saying you're sorry you chose law, are you? I can't imagine another field you'd be as well suited for."

"I'm quite content actually. And you? Any regrets for having chosen to become a teacher?"

She shifted her position, distracted by a hummingbird interested for a moment in her red jacket. "I loved it for the short time I was doing it. I adore children."

"So you're done teaching after just one year? More's the pity I guess, but there's never been a working McLagen wife in recent history, so I suppose you're going to continue with that tradition."

"I can't continue to teach even if I wanted to."

"I'm surprised that my brother hasn't already laid down the law in that regard anyway."

She studied him for a moment. "No one lays down the law to me, Dalton. I have my own mind. This is 1927. Women think for themselves now, modern women that is and I am a modern woman."

He held up both hands in a defensive gesture. "Whoa! You're still a feisty little thing, aren't you?"

She folded her arms, resigned to having this conversation with her future brother-in-law. No matter she wasn't in the mood for it, but she wasn't ready to return home just yet either. Tempers wouldn't have cooled enough, including her own. She'd have walked to Fanny's except she'd gone into Saint John with her aunt and uncle. So here she sat.

"I'm not feisty, I speak my mind is all."

"I applaud that, Miss Estey. It's an admirable quality."

She ignored the compliment. Perhaps if she were cool enough he'd hopefully give up and leave. She remembered just as quickly though that once Dalton sank his teeth into something he wasn't inclined to let go easily. She sensed there was something he was itching to say and sure enough he got right down to it.

"Sarah, I have a question for you. It's one you may think you've already answered, but you haven't. Not to my satisfaction anyway. Why did you let me go before you'd given you and I, us as a couple, a fair chance? I know you said something about compatibility or some such thing, but I figured you were just saying what you thought I needed to hear. Tell me the truth, what did Connor offer you to steal you away like he did? Whatever it is, I'll go him one better if you'll call off the wedding."

"Call off the wedding! Not you too!"

"Me too?"

She wasn't about to reveal what had taken place at her dinner table tonight. But in any event, she knew full well there wasn't a shortage of eligible young women in the area. There were plenty to go around so why was *she* being pestered? First Thomas, and then Dalton. Lovesick fools both of them.

"Now why in the world would I call off the wedding when I'm going to marry the man I love?"

"You didn't answer my question."

"I believe I did, Dalton. Connor didn't offer me anything. You see, it's really very simple. We fell in love. There was a connection between us that wasn't there with you."

"I'm not in the habit of losing out to my brother," he announced, folding his arms firmly across his chest. "We're very competitive you know. It was a real feather in his cap that he was able to take you away from me, and don't think he isn't gloating about doing so."

"Gloating?"

"Yes, gloating. And don't expect me to believe he didn't offer you some sort of incentive."

"I don't think I like what you're insinuating."

"Okay then, I won't insinuate. I don't think I'm telling tales out of school when I say both my mother and father think you're a gold digger. First one McLagen son and then the other. Doesn't that sound a little over-ambitious when I say it out loud?"

"First of all, I know what your mother and father think of me and honestly, it doesn't bother me. I feel sorry for them they can't see what a good person I am. I do wish we could have all gotten along. I was certainly prepared to do so, but I have no control over what other people think. What's really bothering them is that I come from a poor background and that's something *I* have no control over."

He chuckled, seemingly enjoying himself. "You're brave, I'll give you that. Coming into the McLagen family on such a sour note is like heading into a war zone, unarmed. Doesn't sound too smart if you ask me."

She met his sardonic gaze head on. "Oh, I'm armed, don't worry about that. I don't scare easily, Dalton. That's something that's always been in my favour. Like I say I wish it could be another way, but the stage is already set and there's nothing I can do about it. I've tried to befriend your parents, but they aren't interested. So be it."

"I would think if *I* were bringing you into the family as my bride, I'd be doing a much better job of paving the way, but good ole Connor seems content to let the chips fall where they may. He always has been all for himself. You made a serious mistake in judgment when you jumped ship for him. Time will prove me right, you'll see."

She straightened the lapels of her jacket, noticing one was slightly crooked. "Time *will* tell, won't it? I expect Connor and I will have a long, happy life together."

"Dream on, darling, because that's not the way I see it at all. I know Connor. I'm his brother. I grew up with him. He is Mother and Father's pet and they will give him anything he wants, which is why they're indulging him in this. They're hoping, even at this stage, either you or Connor will come to your senses and end this farcical engagement. I guess that would leave Connor to make the break because from where I sit you've got a death grip on that brass ring. It would take a mighty strong tug to get that out of your greedy little hands."

She chuckled derisively. "I'm a terrible person? Greedy? A gold-digger? If that's all true, why are *you* interested in me? If you weren't, you wouldn't be here talking to me right now, would you? Admit it!"

"I do admit it, I've never led you to believe otherwise. The difference is I would talk some sense into you. I would brook no nonsense. I would see to it that you kept your teaching job, pull some strings to make that happen. I would encourage it. Let you pay your way and since you've already indicated that's what you'd like to do anyway, I would say half the battle has already been won. So again, what's the scheme? The Connor I know is more interested in besting me than bedding you, so he must have really sweetened the pot."

She laughed. "No financial incentive, Dalton, if that's what you're implying. You're overthinking things as usual. You see, he didn't need to offer me any incentive, comparing the two of you did the trick. You haven't got half the personality or charm that your brother does. Connor would not need to pay a woman to leave you for him, they'd just do it out of natural inclination."

"You've got a common mouth."

"If that's how you describe a woman with a mind of her own, and not afraid to speak it."

"And what, my dear, is the attraction in that? A wife should stand quietly by her husband's side, not constantly compete for the spotlight. If this wedding goes ahead as planned, Connor will rue the day he ever married you. I see nothing but trouble ahead for him the poor sop."

"But *you* could tame me, is that what you think?"

"You and I are a lot alike, Sarah. I make no apologies for the kind of man I am. Connor is weak. He will never be the success our father was in business. You, Sarah, need someone strong, like me. I see your imperfections, all of them, but I wouldn't let you control me the way Connor will. You're too strong, too much woman for him. Tell me, has he even kissed you the way you were meant to be kissed or is he still playing the perfect gentleman?"

Her face flamed. "That's none of your business."

"Ahh, so he hasn't."

"I don't like what you're saying."

"But I thought we were going to speak our minds, or is it just you that has that privilege?"

"You're loathsome."

He chuckled, and it was a dangerous sound. "Say what you will, but I know you wished you had let me kiss you like that when you had the chance. I tried on more than one occasion if you recall, and you always played the innocent."

"I never played the innocent!" she stated indignantly, realizing at once that she had willingly stepped into his trap. "I mean...."

Dalton threw back his head and laughed. "Now we're getting somewhere. I knew with a little prodding the real Sarah would show her hand. Oh, how I wish I had kissed you properly. It's not like you wouldn't have known how." He shook his head. "And now all of that is going to be wasted on my weak little brother. What a pity. You may be wrapped up in a small package, Sarah, but you're all woman. You're exactly what I need in my life."

"I don't want to be part of your life. I already have everything I need in my own."

"You have what you think you need in your life. You're settling for a bank account, but you'll fall short in the bedroom. I guarantee it. I think of you and I together. I would make your blood boil, Sarah. And you wouldn't exactly be poor. It's a win/win situation as far as I can see and if you weren't so stubborn, choosing a man you can wrap around your little finger, then you'd admit it."

"I'll admit no such thing. You are beastly!"

Dalton laughed again. "Honesty has its price."

"This wedding will take place just as we've planned it," she told him. "Connor and I will be very good together and that's what you can't stand. You lost and you're choking on sour grapes."

His smile never reached his eyes. "Is that what it is? Tell me, Sarah, how do your parents feel about the upcoming nuptials? Something tells me there's been a row, or you wouldn't be sitting here at this hour on a school night."

"It's early yet, the sun won't even be going down for another hour and a half. As usual, you're completely off base."

"Am I? Can you sit there and tell me your parents are in favour of you marrying my brother? Think long and hard before you answer because he and I have already talked about this."

"All right, they don't like it, okay? But then again, they're not in favour of me marrying a McLagen at all, you included. They think that name carries a bad reputation, and they don't want mine ruined."

"Everyone knows my old man is a crook, it's not exactly a secret. But he's a rich crook and at the end of the day it's what's in the bank that matters. We have never wanted for anything. Besides, he doesn't harm anyone. He does what's best for the company, not that I expect you to understand that in your sheltered little world of right and wrong, good and evil."

"I come from a good home, an honest home. My parents only want what's best for me."

"Really? They'd prefer you to sit home and become an old maid? Keep you locked up in the attic until you're too old and ugly for any man to want you?"

She turned to face him. "For your information, they have someone in mind for me to marry. His name is Thomas Chaffee and he's a missionary in The Belgian Congo ... that's in Africa in case you wondered."

He chuckled again. "I excelled in geography, but thanks for the information. So what's the deal? You would become a missionary too?"

"A teaching missionary, yes."

Dalton laughed long and hard. "Now that I'd like to see. You're no more cut out to become a missionary than I am. You're too greedy, too devious."

"Once again, if you have such a poor opinion of me, why do you want me?"

"Because like I said, we're perfectly matched. I like your spice, little Sarah. You'd never get the better of me, but you'd keep things interesting."

"It's too bad I don't want you then. The truth of it is I'm in love with your brother. I am going to marry him, and that's the end of it."

"Really? The end of it?"

"Yes."

"And do you think Connor is being faithful to you?"

"Connor doesn't have a dishonourable bone in his body."

He smiled. "Right. Well, your honourable little fiancé is, as we speak, visiting with the lovely Gladys Biddington. In case that name doesn't ring a bell, she's his former girlfriend. They had planned to marry until you came along. We all hoped they would because she's a much better choice for him than you are."

"You're lying!"

"I'm not lying. I asked where Connor was earlier, and my mother told me that Gladys called for him and asked that he return the call. But instead of doing that, he decided to go and pay her a visit in person. I haven't seen my mother so happy in a long while. I'd say she has her fingers crossed that Connor comes to his senses and marries Gladys. She's the daughter of family friends and we all adore her. If you think you've got this all sewed up in a tidy little bundle, think again. Happily engaged men, men who are counting the hours until they can get to the church don't go calling on old girlfriends for any reason."

Sarah felt shock dash through her and she struggled to keep it off her face. Connor was at Gladys Biddington's? Was this the first time or had it been going on for a while and she'd been too blinded by love to notice?

"Sorry to have to hurt you like that, Sarah. Better your eyes be opened now than later, and this isn't the first time he and Gladys have gotten together. Far from it."

Chapter Five

"How dare you tell a lie like that, Dalton! Connor is not seeing Gladys Biddington behind my back. He wouldn't! You'll stop at nothing to get what you want, will you?"

Dalton held up his hands in an exaggerated defensive gesture. "Don't shoot the messenger, Sarah. Believe me, he *is* with Gladys Biddington tonight. Then again, he's not married yet so I guess he's just sowing a few more wild oats. He wouldn't be the first."

"I don't believe you, how's that for some wild oats? I'm not that easily taken in," she lied, her stomach clenched at the news of Connor's possible infidelity.

Had she really been that stupid? She'd trusted him implicitly. She'd always been aware of her power over him, enjoying the fact he was so enamoured with her but had his parents finally succeeded in driving a wedge between them? Convinced Connor to return to his former girlfriend whom she knew had the more desirable pedigree? She, Sarah, had no pedigree at all, a schoolteacher and the daughter of a pastor, poor as a church mouse.

He shrugged again. "Believe what you like, but your lap dog is not as obedient as you thought he was. Better to find that out now than later I should think. Come on, I'll drive you home, unless you plan to sit here on these steps all night. It'll be dark in a half hour."

"I can walk, thank you," she shot back.

"Not a good idea. Why, anything could happen to a woman on the road alone … especially with it getting dark and all. Come on, Sarah, your feet must be sore already from walking here in those heels. Your shoes look mighty uncomfortable to me, even to sit in."

She looked away. "They got me here and they can get me back."

"Don't be so stubborn, let me drive you. I don't bite, but then you already know that."

She thought of the walk home. Her poor feet were hurting unbearably. She loved these shoes, but they did pinch and she had been on her feet all day. *She* might be disinclined to accept the offer of a drive, but her feet were very much in favour of it.

"Oh, all right," she said ungraciously. "I'll let you drive me home."

"Isn't that generous of you! I have a mind to rescind the offer."

"Okay, I'm sorry. Yes, Dalton, I would appreciate a drive home."

"That's more like it. I'm sure you can stand my company for a few more minutes."

It was barely a ten-minute drive although it would likely take longer considering Dalton didn't seem inclined to make proper use of the accelerator. They were underway for less than a minute when they met an automobile coming the other way. Connor! Dalton flashed his brother a Cheshire cat smile and a friendly wave as the two cars passed each other at slow speed in the fading light. Sarah's heart fell right into her shoes and stayed there. Of all people to see them together. Why hadn't she walked back instead! Confound that Dalton, he probably had a good idea they'd meet Connor on the road, but then how would he know the exact minute Connor would be leaving for home?

Nevertheless, the damage had been done and Dalton was soon pulling into the long driveway leading to the parsonage. He stopped the car a short distance from the house and turned off the ignition as Sarah reached for the door handle.

"Just a minute, Sarah."

She stopped and turned toward him. "Yes? What else could you possibly have to say to me? Another revelation about how terrible Connor is? Or how I would be much better off if I had stayed with you? Don't bother, I'm not going to pay any attention to anything else you have to say to me."

Dalton looked chastened. "I just want to apologize for perhaps being a little too honest. I figure the wedding is going to go ahead anyway, no matter what I say and no matter what Connor does. I'm sorry to have upset you."

She hesitated. It wasn't like Dalton to apologize. That had taken her completely by surprise. "All right, I also said some mean things. Apology accepted. I'm sorry too."

He smiled. "No sense in us being at odds, is there? We're going to be family. We should try to get along."

A shadow of a smile touched her lips. She did not like Dalton, but for the sake of maintaining peace in both families she would accept the olive branch he was extending to her.

"I agree, Dalton. We can at least be civil to each other. There's nothing to be gained from bickering. There's already been enough of that anyway with both families opposed to Connor and I getting married. I don't know why in heaven's name this has caused such a stir. People fall in love every day and get married."

He nodded; she could see it despite the fact dusk was steadily gathering around them. "I've made it plain, Sarah, that I'd hoped things could have gone another way for you and me, but I accept your decision. You are a very beautiful woman, and I can't imagine there's only been Connor and I panting after you. You have to expect the loser to be disappointed. Can't you find it in your heart to be more gracious about that?"

"Yes," she murmured noncommittally, shifting uncomfortably. "I must get in now, Dalton. Thank you for the drive. It was kind of you to do that."

"And kind of you to accept I believe I should add," he chuckled then suddenly covered the distance between them, his mouth descending on hers in a rough demanding kiss, his hands holding her head in place. She tasted blood.

Wrenching away she struck out at him. Her hand connected with his face, her diamond ring inflicting a deep cut on his upper lip. "How dare you!" she seethed, groping for the door handle.

Dalton already had a handkerchief to his mouth as he grabbed her arm in a punishing grip. "Listen you little bitch...."

"Get your hand off me, you animal!" she seethed. "You let me go this instant or I'll scream, and you'll have my father to contend with!"

"No one strikes me and gets away with it, Sarah," he said, deadly calm. "Not even you. You're going to be one sorry young woman."

* * *

Sarah was badly shaken as she slammed the car door and headed for the house on the run, pinched toes and all. It wasn't that she thought Dalton would exert himself to catch her, but she knew now what he was capable of, and it frightened her. She breathed a sigh

91

of relief as she watched his hasty retreat down the driveway and took a few minutes to collect herself before going inside.

Her mother was sitting at the kitchen table her eyes red from crying. Thankfully Thomas Chaffee was nowhere to be seen, and she was at least grateful for that.

She sat down across from her mother, reaching to take her hand. "Mother, I hate to see you so upset."

Maude lifted weary eyes to her daughter. "This whole marriage business has been very upsetting, Sarah. You won't listen to reason. You're pushing your father and I beyond all endurance. I've never seen him so angry. He's gone out, in case you're wondering where he is."

"Where did Daddy go?"

"Beaumont Ainsley called for him about a half hour ago. It seems Polly Ainsley won't last the night before she crosses over Jordan, and they want your father there when she passes away."

"So he'll likely be with the family all night."

Her mother nodded, the cup of tea in front of her having long since gone cold. "I expect so, and him so furious with you he's beside himself. You know, Sarah, you might consider the feelings of other people before you rush headlong into whatever scheme comes into your head. All we've ever wanted for you was to make decisions that will serve you well your entire life. I don't think I need to remind you one bad choice can spoil all your chances for happiness. I want you to be happy, Sarah."

She held onto her mother's hand, caressing the rough skin with the pad of her thumb. "I am happy, Mother," she said although, try as she might, she couldn't push Dalton's revelations about Connor from her mind. "I'm sure you know what it's like to be in love, to want to get married. Isn't that how you felt when you met Daddy? Isn't that all you could think about? Your life together? Your future? You made your choice. Allow me to make mine."

Maude squeezed her eyes shut as though to block out disturbing memories. "Sarah, I'm going to tell you something that in the normal course of events would be none of your affair. If it will help in this situation, I'll share a secret with you."

Sarah's stomach took a second nosedive within the hour. Now what?

"All right, what's the secret?" she asked with trepidation.

"I guess if I'm being honest there are two secrets."

Her mother began to speak then hesitated as if to summon the courage to continue.

"Sarah," she said finally, "I never had any say in who I married, everything was arranged by my parents. They promised me to your father when I was sixteen and he's almost fourteen years older than me. I believed I had no choice but to go along with it. I don't have your spunk, my dear. Your father is a highly respected minister and I've tried to make peace with the rest."

She was shocked as she studied her mother's face with new eyes. "Have you ever been happy?" she asked gently.

Her mother returned her gaze. "Is that a fair question to ask do you think? We had you to raise and there were certainly good times when you were a child."

Sarah grimaced. "Not so much after I began to grow up, I guess. I admit I can be very headstrong."

Maude smiled, fleetingly, and even that tiny gesture was transformative. "You've certainly been a handful, but I love you."

"*You* love me."

"Your father doesn't love easily. It's not in his nature."

"I've noticed that."

"Sarah! You were taught to respect your elders."

"You say you had no choice as to who you married, and now you're trying to do the same by forcing Thomas Chaffee on me. Don't you see? I know it's mostly Daddy, but why would you go along with him? You know it's wrong."

Maude stared at the table. "I know," she said, her voice barely a whisper. "I should have been stronger through this whole thing, but the McLagens scare me." She raised her eyes. "Your father scares me."

Sarah wisely did not comment on that particular statement, returning out of curiosity to her mother's earlier remark. "You said you had me to raise. What does that mean? Is that the second secret you're about to tell me?"

Maude lowered her head again. "Yes," she said quietly. "That's the other secret."

She braced herself. "I don't belong to you and Daddy, do I?"

"Of course you belong to us!"

"What I mean to say is you're not my natural parents are you?"

Maude exhaled, a sigh likely pent up for a lifetime. "No, we're not. A girl in our church, a wayward girl named Winifred Collicut became pregnant, and her parents did not want to send her away, nor did they want the child. So she had the baby, a beautiful little girl and we adopted her. That was you and I've never been sorry we did that, not for one moment."

"Is that why Daddy doesn't care for me? I'm from what he would call a bad seed?"

"Since I'm being honest, you're closer to the truth than you know. He tried to counsel that girl, but she wouldn't listen. She was very headstrong, stubborn. He sees in you what he saw in her, and it frustrates him."

Sarah felt as though she'd been knocked sideways. She'd always wondered why she didn't resemble either her mother or father, never once guessing at the truth of things. "Where is my real mother now?"

Maude pushed her cold cup of tea further to the side. "Scattered to the wind."

"What does that mean, scattered to the wind?"

"It means she went the way of the world. She hadn't seen her parents in years before they were informed she'd taken her own life. I'm sorry, Sarah. I know she was your natural mother, but she had no inclination to raise you. She was only interested in herself and fulfilling her own pleasures. It's not a pretty story but I felt you had a right to know. I know you feel we've not been good parents, but if it wasn't for us, you would have been placed in an orphanage and neither of us wanted that for you. We're not wealthy people like the McLagens, but we're honest and hardworking and we have always tried to do our best for you."

This must be what it felt like to be poleaxed. "I thank you for that, and now I have to do what's best for me, for all of us. I appreciate what you and Daddy have done for me, given me, but that duty is done now. I will make my own decisions."

"It wasn't just duty, Sarah. I thought you would have understood that. You are as much my child as if I had given birth to you. Now, I've told you things I probably shouldn't have, and I will ask you to keep those secrets."

She squeezed her mother's hand again. "I'll keep the secrets, Mother. You have my word."

Maude cocked her head, listening. "I hear someone in the yard. Mrs. Ainsley must have passed away sooner than expected and your father's home already."

Just then a sharp knock came to the door and Sarah rose quickly to answer it. She somehow wasn't surprised to see Connor standing under the porch lamp where a June bug flew in haphazard circles, dazzled by the light.

He was the first to speak. "Sarah, can you come for a drive with me? You and I need to talk."

She could see even by the dim glow he was flushed, a man with something on his mind and she knew what it was about. Dalton. Would this night never end?

"It's a school night, Connor, and I have to get up early. I know you do too, but certainly, we can talk for a few minutes." She slipped back into her jacket. "I'll step out with you for a moment."

"I thought we could go out to the Point in my car. We could have privacy there," he said, looking pointedly beyond Sarah where her mother was gazing in their direction, clearly curious.

Sarah shrugged. "We could do that, as long as it's only for a few minutes."

Neither said a word during the drive to the Point. Connor pulled into their usual spot next to the landing, shut off the engine and then turned in the seat to face her.

"I want an explanation, Sarah, and I want it right now. Are you seeing Dalton behind my back?"

Naturally he'd want to know why she was in Dalton's vehicle, and it could be easily explained, but this? "Me seeing Dalton behind your back? Are you serious, Connor? Of course not!"

"You two looked mighty cozy driving down the road together. Everyone could see you. I told you I was not going to let you make a fool of me any more than you already have. I'm serious about that, deadly serious."

"What is that supposed to mean?"

"Exactly what you think it means. How long have you two been carrying on together?"

"Connor, this is ridiculous! I went for a walk and was sitting on the steps of Saint Paul's and who should come along but Dalton. He came to sit beside me, and we talked for a few minutes. Then since it was coming on dark, he offered me a drive home. I should think you'd rather him do that than have me walking the road at night, alone."

She decided in that moment to spare him the details of the set-to. There was already enough animosity between the families, and he and his brother in particular. She refused to be the catalyst for more. Besides, she wasn't a tattletale and she'd taken care of the situation herself. Let Dalton explain how he'd gotten a bloody lip. That would teach him to keep *his* to himself.

Her explanation quieted him for a moment, but only that. "I don't like seeing the two of you together. You know I'm having trust issues with you, Sarah, and just when I start to feel better, I see *that*. It did seem as though you were sitting awfully close."

"Where should I have been sitting, on the roof? I hope you know how silly you sound. But if you need to hear me say it, then no, I have no interest in Dalton other than a drive home. I don't care for your brother. I think you already know that. It's you I love and that's all I'm going to say about it. Now," she said, squaring her shoulders, "I heard you paid Gladys Biddington a visit tonight. I will ask you the same question, are you seeing her behind *my* back?"

He settled deeper into the seat, suddenly it seemed at a loss for words. "I did go and see Gladys tonight," he said at length. "She called me this afternoon and left a message with Mother, so I decided to go after dinner and find out what she wanted. We'd have more privacy that way."

"Privacy! To do what?"

"To have a conversation. That's all."

"Why was she calling you in the first place may I ask?"

He turned to look at her again, but it was a moment before he spoke. "She's still in love with me, Sarah. She called to see if I could give her another chance."

"I'm sure she knows you're engaged to me and I'm also sure she knows we are to be married in a matter of days. Or did that subject come up?"

"Certainly it came up. She knows about you."

"I should think so. Rothesay is a very small place, even smaller when you consider gossip. It must have been a long conversation. You say you went there after dinner, and we met you coming home just before dark. How long does it take to say you're in love with someone else, going to marry them in fact? To tell her there would be no second chance. There, I've just said it and it took about ten seconds ... maybe less."

"Gladys is still a good friend."

"How good, Connor? Is there something you'd like to say to me? Are you having second thoughts about us?"

He took too long to answer in her estimation as he stared out over the river.

"I'm not getting cold feet if that's what you're asking." He puffed out a breath. "Maybe everyone has doubts ...."

"Doubts! Connor McLagen, do you want to marry me or not?"

He ran his hand through his hair. "Maybe I just want to get it over with!"

"Get it over with! Get what over with?"

"The whole church thing, the day, the ceremony. All of that is nerve-wracking. I'll probably settle in all right once all of the hoopla is over and done with and we're away on our honeymoon. I *am* looking forward to the honeymoon."

"Your enthusiasm for our wedding day is overwhelming. I thought you were looking forward to having me walk down the aisle to you. I seem to recall you saying as much in your toast speech."

He laid his head back. "I am looking forward to that, Sarah. But I'll be honest with you, I'm not looking forward to having your father glaring daggers at me the whole time. No offence, but the less I see of him the better."

"So, Connor, tell me truly. Are you having doubts about marrying *me*? Do you wish you were marrying Gladys instead? There'd be a honeymoon to look forward to there too since that's what you're so hepped up about."

He was quiet, the mournful call of a loon out on the water a fitting punctuation for the silence in the car. "I do wonder if we moved too quickly, although it's been a whole year now. No, it's you I love, Sarah. Don't pay any attention to me. It's just last-minute jitters. Everyone gets them."

"Dalton said you've seen Gladys several times."

"Dalton is not telling the truth, as usual. This was the first time I've seen her since you and I've been together."

"And when will you be seeing her again?"

"Sarah...."

"I asked you a question."

"My mother wants me to invite her to dinner and if she accepts it would be rude of me to not be there when she's our guest. It wouldn't mean anything though. Honestly."

* * *

The next day was a busy one. There was a school picnic for the children, which Sarah had helped organize and it was a resounding success. Additionally there were still personal details to be seen to in preparation for the wedding and Fanny was only too happy to help. Her best friend had even borrowed the estate's work vehicle utilized by her Uncle Frederick in his position as caretaker. He'd taught his niece how to drive so the two young women were off on a lark giggling like schoolgirls as they motored into Saint John to attend to Sarah's errands.

* * *

It was now three days before the wedding and Reverend Estey was no more in favour of it now than he had been at the outset. Maude, for her part, remained silent on the subject. Last night had been especially tense. About mid-evening Thomas Chaffee had arrived at the back door, visibly upset, and needing to speak to Reverend Estey immediately. Minutes later Cranston announced he had to drive Thomas into

Saint John at once and it had been late when he returned to the parsonage.

Cranston was still in a surly mood this morning. "Look at this, Maude," he said as he snapped open the newspaper at the breakfast table. "They've got that Madawaska gangster in court up in Fredericton. If ever there was a scoundrel with this whole Prohibition thing, it's him and his mob. Slippery as an eel, that one. But it looks like the long arm of the law finally caught up with him. It says here he's putting on quite a show in the courtroom and it's making for some great headlines. What some people won't do when it comes to escaping prosecution. Just look what trouble liquor brings with it and that demon rum is the worst in my opinion. But it seems while some are finally brought to justice, there are just as many who aren't. Like that old Pritchard McLagen. Everyone knows he's involved, that he pays off the inspectors. Guilty as sin I tell you, yet he'll slip away too because money talks."

"Now, Cranston."

"Don't you now Cranston me!" he told her impatiently. "Are you siding with the McLagen's now?"

Maude had already begun to wring her hands as she rushed to try to defuse her husband's outburst. "No, I meant I don't want to see you get yourself upset."

"I'll be the judge of that. I shall get upset if that's what the situation calls for and make no apologies to you when I do. Stop fussing!" he admonished when he saw she was about to intervene again.

Maude turned away, as though waiting to be dismissed. "All right, Cranston. It's just that the doctor said...."

He threw down the paper, always ready for a fight. "Don't bring that blame doctor up to me again. There's nothing whatsoever wrong with my heart. I tossed those pills of his away six months ago and I have had not one bit of trouble. It was your idea to call him in the first place and I ought to have made you get a job to pay his bill which in my opinion was outrageous."

She bit off another "Now, Cranston", saying instead: "Would you like a second cup of tea? It's still hot."

He snatched up the paper again, the surly mood he reserved chiefly for his family, not improved. "No, I would not. I have to be on my way. I have a deacons meeting this morning and they're likely already starting to arrive. Except for Donald Livingston. That man will be late for his own funeral."

"All right then, dear, I'll get started on my housework."

"If you dust this furniture anymore, you'll wear it out. Wood can only take so much polishing, but if that's what you want to get to don't let me hold you back."

* * *

It was a relief, as it usually was, when she heard the back door close behind her husband as he headed to the church next door, blessed peace and quiet. After cleaning up the breakfast dishes she laid out the ingredients to make bread then set about tidying. Sarah took care of her own room, but she still liked to run a dust cloth over the furniture, maybe open the windows to let in a little fresh air. With dust cloth in hand, she headed for the back of the house and Sarah's bedroom.

The bed was made and not a thing was out of place, as usual, the window already open. That's when she saw the note sitting on the small table that sat in front of the window. Curiously, it was addressed to her, so she slowly picked it up, aware her hands had begun to tremble.

"Dear Mother, I have changed my mind about marrying Connor. I am leaving town. Please don't try to find me. I love you. Sarah"

Chapter Six

Maude stood shaking, note in hand. Sarah had been with Fanny to Saint John late yesterday afternoon but had planned to be back early in the evening. She'd assumed Sarah had met up with Connor along the way and come in later than usual. Perhaps they'd quarrelled and that's why she'd changed her mind. But if so, why would it be necessary to leave home? Where would she go without any transportation? Had she gone off with someone?

Clutching the note, she hurried out of the house heading for the church at a trot. Cranston's meeting would have already started, but this was urgent. He would understand why it was necessary to be interrupted.

Going in by the back door she headed for the basement, guided to his office by the murmur of men's voices. Clutching the note, she hesitated only a moment before knocking with uncharacteristic sharpness on the heavy wooden door. The voices inside hushed, and she could hear her husband's: "What in thunder!"

Moments later the door was wrenched open, Cranston's eyes widening when he saw his wife. Making his apologies to those in the room, he closed the door behind him and motioned for her to follow him outside, not speaking until they had gained the yard.

"Have you lost your mind, Maude? You know you can't come barging into a meeting like that."

Maude was suddenly past cowering. "I didn't barge in, Cranston, I knocked, and I did so for a very good reason." She thrust the note at him, and he took it from her.

"Finally she's got some sense in her head," he announced after he'd read it. "I'd like to think it's because of what we've been trying to tell her. Now the way is clear for her to marry the Chaffee fellow. But as welcome as this news is, Maude, you needn't have interrupted an important meeting to tell me. It could have waited until I came home at lunchtime. Now go on back to what you were doing and no more wild flights to the church, understood?"

She took the note back from her husband, staring at him wide-eyed. "Cranston, the note says she's left and not to try to find her. But we have to try to find her wherever she's gone. She's alone and probably frightened."

He chuckled, shaking his head. "I doubt that Sarah has ever been frightened, Maude, she's too wilful for that. Go along home like I say. She's probably already there waiting for us." He chuckled derisively. "It doesn't take much to get a rise out of you, does it?"

"Cranston," she persisted worriedly. "We have to find her. Something's wrong, I know it is."

He leaned back on his heels, his hands partway in the front pockets of his trousers. "And just what do you intend to do? She's always been crowing about how grown up she is, was all set to marry that gangster's son in good conscience. This is just another one of her attention-seeking antics. She's already accomplished what she set out to do which is to get you worked up, but I'm not so easily gotten because I know her. I know her kind. Don't worry your head about it, she'll be home by suppertime."

The note stuffed in the pocket of her checkered apron, Maude had begun to wring her hands, on the verge of tears. "But, Cranston...."

It was apparent he had reached the limit of his patience, fire flashing in his eyes. "Do not make me raise my voice, Maude. I told you to go home and I expect you to do it. I've already listened to as much of this foolishness as I intend to. She says she's changed her mind about marrying a McLagen and I say Halleluiah if that's the end of it. Now go back to the parsonage. I have no more time at the moment to deal with any of this. Do as I tell you!"

Maude felt the sting of her husband's scolding as she headed back to the parsonage. Tears threatened but she would not shed them in the churchyard in front of anyone who might happen by. Maybe Cranston was right. Maybe Sarah would come home with an explanation for what she'd written. But in her heart, she remained unsettled. Could her husband not see this was out of character for their daughter? It was true Sarah could be impetuous, but she was also responsible. This was a workday and unless she was already at school it meant she'd left her class without a teacher.

She looked at the clock. Ten forty-five. Cranston wouldn't be home for lunch until twelve-thirty, sharp, so she had time if she left soon to walk up to the school and see if Sarah was there. She'd have to move quickly though. Changing out of her kitchen clothes she grabbed a light shift in favour of the warm day and left.

If she hurried, she'd be home in time to have Cranston's lunch on the table. She'd made him a sandwich and put it in the icebox before leaving in case she was a minute or two late. She also knew she would incur his wrath if he knew she'd gone to the school, but she'd made the trip regardless of his inevitable tantrum.

She tried to pace herself so she wouldn't be in a lather by the time she reached the schoolhouse. As she walked, she prayed Sarah would be at school. She'd be relieved if there was no substance to the note, but angry, yes, because she was still badly frightened.

It was just past eleven-thirty when the school came into sight, and she slowed her pace as she approached and climbed the stairs to the front door. She was familiar with the layout of the school having been here before, deciding to wait by the door to speak to the school principal, Miss Martin. That's if she didn't see Sarah first.

On the dot of twelve classes were let out, children filing into the hallway in orderly dismissal. She spied an angular woman in a dark skirt and white blouse with an impossibly high neckline bustling toward her. That must be the principal.

"Miss Martin," she began, stepping forward, "I'm Maude Estey, Sarah's mother. Can you tell me if Sarah came to work this morning? If she's here now?"

It seemed Miss Martin had swallowed something distasteful, given her dour expression. "No, I have not seen Sarah yet this morning and that has left us shorthanded. Is Sarah ill?"

"Ahh no, she's not ill."

"Where is she then? I would like an explanation as to why she failed to turn up for work today."

"I'm very sorry, Miss Martin. I don't believe Sarah will be here today. I apologize on her behalf."

The principal, still stony-faced, acknowledged Maude's response with a curt nod of her head before marching away.

Just then Maude noticed Fanny start in her direction and her spirits lifted at the sight of Sarah's best friend. "Could I speak with you a moment outside, Fanny?" asked Maude.

"Certainly, Mrs. Estey," and the two descended the front stairs and found a quiet spot a short distance away.

"Fanny," Maude began, her voice shaking. "I found a note in Sarah's bedroom this morning that says she's changed her mind about marrying Connor. It also went on to say she's left town and we're not to try to find her. Do you know anything about any of this?"

Fanny took a step back, gaping at her. "She has decided not to marry Connor? Why ever not? That's ludicrous."

"I know nothing other than what I've just told you was written in the note. I've been in a state of shock since I found it. I don't know what to do."

"What about the reverend? What does he think about it?"

"He's glad that Sarah has changed her mind about the wedding. He doesn't think there's anything to worry about with her having said she's going off somewhere."

Fanny was quiet for a moment. "I think if I were in Sarah's shoes, I would do the same thing. I would need time to get myself sorted out. I think Reverend Estey is right. Just leave her alone. If she doesn't want to be found, I would respect that. Sarah has her own mind. She said something once about moving to a big city and seeing what city life is all about. That could be what she's done."

Maude shook her head. "I'm afraid it doesn't make sense to me. Why would she leave without saying good-bye? You two are close friends, wouldn't she have told you what she was going to do? Where she was going?"

Fanny shook her head. "You know Sarah. She'd always been so determined. Besides, Mrs. Estey, this is 1927 and Sarah is a modern woman. I would say wherever she is, she's fine. I certainly wouldn't worry."

Maude felt completely adrift. Why wasn't anyone alarmed by Sarah's disappearance? There wasn't any way in the world she would just run away from her responsibilities, her job. She loved the children too much to simply abandon them and go off to be a *modern woman* in some big city. She knew young people today had some crazy ideas, and Sarah was not one to let anything stand in her way once she had set her mind to something, but this was completely odd.

"Fanny, do you honestly think she would be derelict in her duties as a teacher? That would be completely irresponsible. Her behaviour is most alarming."

Fanny nodded. "I agree. Sarah would never walk away from her teaching responsibilities no matter what decision she had made or how upset she was. But deciding not to marry Connor has likely thrown her off balance a bit and she's not thinking clearly."

"Didn't the two of you go into Saint John yesterday to run some errands for the wedding?"

"Yes, we did. She got shoes from Manchester Robertson, Allison's ... MRA's. You know, that's a beautiful store. They have everything there anyone could possibly want. I saw so many things I would love to have, but on a teacher's salary. Maybe someday."

"Fanny! Where's Sarah? You know where she is, don't you?"

Fanny was already shaking her head. "All I know is we had a quick trip to Saint John and returned in the early evening. If I knew where she went after that I'd tell you, Mrs. Estey. Honestly, I would. You know Sarah, she could change her mind on a dime, and I think that's just exactly what she's done. There were so many people against the wedding I think she'd just had enough. She was probably upset so she packed a few things in a suitcase and got away somewhere. If she said she didn't want to be found, I would take it to mean she'd like to have some time to herself to think about what to do next. I would let her have the time

113

she needs to get over this and she'll be back, happy as ever. Now if you'll excuse me, Miss Martin asked me to speak to her before classes resume after lunch." She stepped closer to Maude. "She'll be back, Mrs. Estey. Try not to worry."

Maude made it home not three minutes before Cranston walked in the back door. He stopped up short when he saw her rushing about the kitchen, hurrying to fill the teakettle and setting out his lunch on the table.

"Why are you looking so windblown, Maude? Where else have you been dashing off to this morning?"

She finished spooning tealeaves into the crockery teapot. "I just got back from the school. I wanted to see if Sarah went to work today."

"You what!"

"I went up to the school to see...."

"I heard you. I just can't believe you'd do something like that. Do you want everyone asking questions about our daughter? You are to keep family matters private, Maude. You're acting just as featherbrained as Sarah, and I won't have it."

She continued on as though he hadn't spoken. "She did not turn up for class, and she would never neglect her responsibilities like that. I tell you something is wrong, Cranston. We have to start looking for her."

"Have you taken complete leave of your senses? She said in her note she was calling off the wedding or something to that effect, isn't that correct?"

"She said she had decided not to marry Connor."

"Don't you see? She finally came to her senses, and she just needed to go off somewhere and lick her wounds. The last thing she would want is you running around the neighbourhood like a ninny involving everyone in our private lives. If you care so much about your daughter, you would do as she asks and leave her alone."

She poured boiling water into the teapot and set it on the back of the stove to steep. "I have a terrible feeling about this, Cranston. I feel she's in trouble."

"Did you see Fanny at the school? She teaches there as well, doesn't she?"

"Yes, I spoke with Fanny."

"And what did she say? Does she know where Sarah went flitting off to?"

"She wasn't even aware Sarah had changed her mind about marrying Connor."

"She probably didn't think she needed to announce it to all and sundry."

"To answer the second part of your question, she has no idea either where she might have gone. But she says the same thing you do. Not to worry. Sarah will be back."

"There you go! Maude, you do have a tendency to go off half-cocked sometimes. Just leave well enough alone. I assume you checked and saw that her suitcase was gone. She's just left for a few days, that's all. She can make her own amends to the school for being absent. She's probably there right now, apologizing. She likely stayed with a friend last night."

Maude laid out the sandwich, saw to Cranston's tea and fetched a jam tart for dessert, pleading no appetite when he asked why she wasn't joining him. Instead, she headed down the hall to see if indeed Sarah's suitcase was gone. She'd not thought to do that she'd been so upended by the note. Maybe Cranston and Fanny were right. Sarah had gone off for a few days to settle her mind and think about her future, one apparently without Connor in it. Both families had been so down on her about the wedding, and Sarah may have just snapped under the pressure. One never knew.

She went into Sarah's room and with hands that had not stopped trembling since the discovery of the note, opened the closet door. Her hand flew to her mouth, stifling a sob when she saw Sarah's beige striped suitcase sitting off to the side beside shoes and a spare handbag. In fact, it didn't appear as though anything had been taken from the closet, even the MRA bags containing her bridal shoes and other items were still on the floor beside the small table where she'd found the note. Her daughter was not exactly a clotheshorse, choosing instead simple frocks, skirts, and blouses. However, virtually everything she'd ever seen her daughter wear was still hanging in the closet.

116

She then went to the chest of drawers and slowly opened each drawer. Sarah, as was typical of an only child, was neat to the point of obsession. Everything was folded and in its usual place. If she had gone off as claimed in her note, she had done it with only the clothes on her back. Even her housecoat was hanging on a hook by her bed, her nightdress folded neatly beneath her pillow. Her hairbrush and other toiletries were sitting on the bureau. Maude truly did feel sick to her stomach now.

Cranston was chewing a mouthful of sandwich when she hurried back into the kitchen. He looked up dispassionately as though surprised to find her still upset.

She had begun to wring her hands. "Cranston, everything Sarah owns is in her bedroom."

He swallowed what he'd been chewing. "What does that tell you, Maude? Hmm?"

"It tells me something's wrong."

"No, what it should tell you is Sarah is being her usual impulsive self. She's run off without a thought to packing a suitcase and taking along what she'd need for this little impromptu holiday. She's probably sitting somewhere right now, miserable, and without the nerve to come back home and face us after writing such a childish note. I say leave her where she is and let her stew in her own juice for a while. When she's had enough of herself, she'll be along. You mark my words. Now I've heard enough about this."

Maude tried with great effort to keep her anxiety in check. It wouldn't solve anything to become hysterical, even though every fibre of her being was screaming at her to find her daughter. As she had told Sarah just the other night, she may not have birthed her, but she was her mother in every other way and her motherly instincts were strong.

"We have to notify Connor she has decided not to marry him. We can at least extend that courtesy."

"Why should it be up to us to do that? I would assume she's already done so. He's probably home crying in his soup right now. He'd be the first person she'd tell, wouldn't it?"

"But what if she hasn't told him? What if he still thinks the wedding is on?"

"Then that would be a sad state of affairs, but it's not something I'm going to spend any time worrying about. I think you'll find Sarah has finally realized she was wrong and changed her mind about not wanting to marry Thomas. Do you recall I sent him after her the night he was here, and she so childishly went storming out? Does that sound familiar to you? Sarah running away when the water got a bit too warm. Anyway, we have no idea what he may have said to her, but it must have done some good. He's made her listen to reason is what he's done. It was something we as her parents were not able to accomplish, but if Thomas has, then more power to him. There's going to be a wedding all right, and this time it will be something we can truly celebrate."

Maude sat down heavily at the table, dropping her head into her hands. "I'd like to think you're right, Cranston, but it doesn't have the ring of truth to it. I can't see her making such an abrupt change of plans, Connor out, Thomas in. She was in love with Connor."

"The operative word there is *was*. She *was* in love with Connor. You've just said a mouthful," Cranston pointed out. "She obviously decided not to marry that McLagen and thank God for that. It was not a moment too soon. Let the McLagens wallow in the embarrassment of their big social wingding gone bust. That McLagen boy is young. He'll find someone else soon enough. It looks good on them to be on the losing end of things for a change."

She looked up at him with tears in her eyes. "Cranston, you speak about your daughter as though you have no love for her at all."

"We did that child a favour when we took her in, but I see too much of her natural mother in her to feel any sort of real attachment. She is Winifred Collicut over and over, through and through. But never mind my feelings, we've been good to that girl; brought her up right, given her everything we could afford to give and her thanks for that has been to thwart us at every turn. You might ask her where is her love for us? Her gratitude? And now she's gone and pulled this fool stunt. I'll tell you one thing, Thomas may love her and be willing to overlook a lot, but she'll not be able to wind him around her little finger like she has that McLagen boy. The problem is you've always been too lenient with her, Maude. That's why she is the way she is. Spoiled. She has never once given any consideration as to how her actions reflect on us. She is entirely self-centred."

Maude felt her face colour. "I love her, Cranston. I always did my best to make sure she knew that."

"And see where love's got you? She's an ungrateful young woman who flits about as though she doesn't have a brain in her head. I tell you she's exactly like her natural mother. And let me tell you this, Maude. When we do manage to get her married off, she'll be someone else's responsibility then and I'll wash my hands of her."

"Cranston!"

"Don't Cranston me! I don't owe her any apologies, you either."

The tears were flowing now. "Cranston, how can you be so cold? You are a man of God. Where is your compassion?"

"I took the child in, didn't I? It would have been the orphanage for her if I hadn't allowed her to come into my home. I will say you were a good mother to her, but I did not then and do not now wish to be a father. And don't you dare to challenge my walk with God. I answer to Him for my actions, and nobody else. Not even you, Maude. I know I'm strict, but I always do what I think is the proper thing. I'm not a man to be flowery and soft, I know the right way and I do not veer from it. Wherever Sarah is and if something has happened to her, it is a situation of her own making. That, my dear, would be divine intervention and I would never stand in the way of that."

"Cranston, Sarah is gone, and I too am guided by God's word. I feel in my heart that wherever she is and whatever is happening, she needs us. We need to look for her."

He laid the strawberry jam tart he had been about to take a bite out of, back on the plate with a slow and deliberate movement. He then fixed her with one of the coldest glares she'd ever seen cross his face. When he spoke, chills raced up and down her spine.

"Maude, I forbid you to look for Sarah."

She stared back at him, aghast, fighting back tears. "But Cranston...."

"Don't but Cranston me!" he shouted pounding his fist on the small wooden table. "I forbid it!"

* * *

Frost hung in the air at the parsonage for the rest of the day, Maude alternating between tears and hope Sarah would home at any moment and explain her strange absence. She was resolved to call Connor tomorrow if Sarah still hadn't come home. There was always a chance he knew something. She was thankful Cranston had retired to his study to work on his sermon for the following Sunday, glad for the time alone.

Sure enough, just after six o'clock that night there was the sound of an automobile in the yard. 'Thank God! Sarah has come back,' thought Maude as she set down the cup she'd been drying and flung the dishtowel onto the counter. Cranston was right, she was only off with friends, licking her wounds. She breathed a sigh of relief until she heard the knock on the door. Why would Sarah knock?

She fairly flew to the door and yanked it open, ready to take Sarah in her arms after she gave her a motherly scolding. But it was not Sarah standing in the doorway, it was a smiling Connor holding a beautiful bouquet of flowers.

"I've just come by to speak with my fiancé, Mrs. Estey. Can you get her for me?"

Chapter Seven

Maude stared at Connor, open-mouthed. Fiancé! "Sarah isn't here, Connor. Let's step outside for a moment so you and I can talk."

The last thing she needed at this moment was for Cranston to come out of his study and add his outrage to the mix. Seeing a McLagen in his home would do just that.

Connor looked at her curiously as he stepped back, and she pulled the door closed behind her. She directed him to a small white lawn table where each claimed one of the two chairs. Pulling the note from her apron pocket she passed it to him.

He dropped the flowers he'd been carrying onto the ground, blanching as he read what Sarah had written. He looked up at Maude in disbelief. "What's this all about? I don't believe Sarah would write such a thing."

"That's her handwriting, Connor. I found it in her bedroom this morning while I was cleaning." Tears threatened again. "I've been in a state of shock ever since."

It appeared as though he was trying to keep his emotions in check. "Which part are you in shock about, Mrs. Estey? I'm aware that neither you nor the reverend wanted us to get married." He studied her for a moment, eyes narrowed. "I think you've sent her off somewhere. You'd do anything to keep us apart once you saw she was going to go through with it."

She could understand his anger because she and Cranston had made no secret of how they felt about the wedding, but to be accused of this! "We've done no such thing, Connor, I can assure you. It's true we were not in favour of the marriage, but...."

"Because she was too good for me. Is that it?"

Maude shook her head. "It's that your backgrounds were too different, that's what concerned us. But we wouldn't have tried to stop the wedding in this way. We had hoped that Sarah would break the engagement, but do it decently."

Connor had regained some of his colour. "So Sarah has conveniently left town, has she? Funny, she went for a dress fitting a few days ago and was picking up her shoes yesterday. Why do you imagine she would suddenly up and change her mind? It's only been a couple of days since I've seen her, and everything was fine then. It just doesn't add up. I think you know exactly where she is."

Maude leaned forward for emphasis. "Can't you see, Connor? I'm as upset about this as you are, but there's been no nefarious plan to hide her away so she can't marry you. That's absurd."

His breathing had begun to quicken as he looked at the parsonage pointedly. "I think she's in the house, maybe even locked away in the attic for all I know."

Maude was aghast. "For one thing there's no attic in the house, only a narrow crawl space and for another you're being ridiculous. We would never do such a thing, no matter how we felt about the wedding."

"Okay then, she's in a closet." He leapt to his feet. "Maybe she's just hiding out while you do her dirty work for her. I'm going in there right now and find her, confront her to see if she actually did write that note. I'm not being put off," he added when Maude also jumped up.

Maude was at his heels as he started for the house. If he went inside in this state of mind, he'd run smack dab into Cranston and there would be fireworks for sure.

"Connor, you can't go in there! Stop! Please!"

"Why? Because I might find her? No, you're not stopping me. I'll get a constable if I have to. I'm not leaving until I have this out with her."

She managed to get ahead of him. "Connor, please," she implored, taking hold of his arm. "We haven't done anything like you suggest to try to prevent the wedding. If I knew where she was at this moment I would tell you, but I don't."

"You're lying."

"I'm not lying!" she hissed, trying to keep her voice low to avoid disturbing Cranston.

"Let me go, Mrs. Estey," he said shaking off her hand and trying to step past her.

"You will have Reverend Estey to contend with if you go in there."

"I'm not afraid of him."

'You should be,' she felt like saying but didn't. "Look, you have to settle down. Reverend Estey is in his study preparing his sermon. I will take you into the house and show you Sarah is not there, you don't need to go charging in like a raging bull. I realize you're upset, but we should be thinking about finding Sarah and making sure she's all right, not carrying on like this. Now if you promise me you'll stay calm, I'll take you indoors."

He appeared to be holding his temper with an effort. "Let me see for myself she's not inside and I'll leave quietly. I give you my word."

He followed her into the small house, and she took him straight to Sarah's room and showed him where she'd found the note.

Connor allowed Maude to escort him from room to room and although he hesitated in front of the door identified as the reverend's study he did not attempt to enter. Indeed, he did peer into the crawl space with a flashlight, apparently satisfying himself that Sarah had not been stowed away among the cobwebs.

When he finally left after a half hour Maude felt drained. It was now painfully obvious Sarah had not told Connor about her change of plans. She had left it to fall back into her parents' laps and at that moment she was very angry with her daughter. In addition to anger was that awful feeling all was not well, and her stomach churned. Where on earth was she?

Her insides clenched even tighter when she heard the door to the study open minutes later and Cranston come marching out. "Did I hear voices?" he asked sharply.

"It was Connor McLagen looking for Sarah."

He stopped in his tracks. "Connor McLagen was in this house? Is that what you're telling me?"

"That's what I'm telling you. He came with a bouquet of flowers for Sarah, and I was the one who had the terrible job of informing him about her change of heart. I actually felt sorry for the poor boy."

"Why didn't you come and get me?"

"I know you don't like to be disturbed when you're preparing your sermon. At first, he believed we were behind all of this. He demanded to be shown through the house to see for himself she wasn't being kept from him. It was dreadful. I felt like a common criminal."

"You should have come and gotten me, woman! Why would you take it upon yourself to deal with this on your own? He wouldn't have gotten in this house if *I'd* answered the door, I can tell you that."

She began to wring her hands. "I was trying to avoid a possible altercation between you two, that's why. I know how you feel about him, and I didn't want the two of you to be together, not in his frame of mind … and yours."

"So I assume he left satisfied she wasn't being held against her will? Good heavens!"

"He left quietly when he saw she wasn't here. I had held out hope that perhaps he might know where she is, but he was just as much taken by surprise as we were. I tell you, Cranston, I'm becoming more terrified by the moment. We have to involve the police. Something has happened to our daughter."

"No! No police!"

"Cranston, please!"

"Don't raise your voice to me, Maude. I won't stand for it in my own home. You are surely trying my patience."

"I *will* raise my voice! Sarah is missing!"

"Listen to you! You're getting yourself all worked up into hysterics over nothing. I tell you she's just gone off for a day or so. She'll be back."

She shook her head, undeterred. "I think you're wrong. I don't believe she's just run off somewhere. A woman wouldn't leave without a change of clothes or her toiletries.

It doesn't make sense she's disappeared into thin air. I don't believe she would change her mind at the last minute either, just to suit us. She loves that boy. She was counting the days to be married to him."

"I'm not going to discuss this with you until you've calmed down. And I would ask you to remember yourself. It would be a mistake to defy me, Maude."

She didn't budge. "I don't see it as defying you, Cranston. That is not my intention. But for the life of me I don't see why you're not as alarmed as I am."

"I look at it as a direct answer to prayer is why, and that's how you should see it too. We're no longer going to be tied to the McLagens. Having them as in-laws would have been disastrous for my reputation, not to mention Sarah carrying that awful name ... *and* her children. It would have been an intolerable situation."

Bowing her head Maude doubled her fists and rested them against her forehead in frustration, dropping her hands before raising her eyes to him again. "You're not going to help me look for her, are you?"

"No, I certainly am not and as I recall I have forbidden you to carry on like this. I would suggest you settle down and accept things as they are."

* * *

Connor pushed his automobile as fast as it would go back up the road, nearly overturning as he cut the wheel into the circular drive to the McLagen estate and braked sharply. The driver's door barely withstood the slam he gave it as he got out and strode for the house. He found his mother and Dalton enjoying a glass of sherry in the living room, his father preferring his usual cup of tea.

Connor marched up to Dalton who was sitting on the sofa and grabbing him by the lapels of his beige linen blazer, hauled him to his feet. "Where is she? What have you done with her?"

Dalton tried to free himself from his brother who bested him by several inches. "Have you lost your mind? What have I done with who?"

Connor held on tightly. "Sarah! What have you done with her? Where are you keeping her?"

Dalton struggled to break Connor's hold, but he was no match for his angry sibling. "I have absolutely no idea what you're talking about. I would assume she's home with her mother and father. That's where she lives, isn't it? Where else would she be?"

Connor didn't budge. "They don't seem to know where she is, that's what I'm talking about. Sarah left a note saying the wedding's off and she's left town. I saw it with my own eyes."

Agnes and Pritchard were now on their feet too, Pritchard trying to pull Connor off his brother, but to no avail.

Dalton wasn't backing down, despite the fact he was obviously at his brother's mercy. "You let go of me, you Neanderthal."

Pritchard gave one almighty tug and managed to separate the two brothers. "Settle down, Connor! What is the meaning of coming in here and attacking your brother like this? Calm down for pity's sake."

Connor's chest was heaving. "He stole my bride," he said, jabbing a forefinger against Dalton's chest. "He couldn't stand to see me get the girl. He's always gotten everything he ever wanted, but I got Sarah and it's eating him up. And now he's convinced her not to marry me, and he's hidden her away somewhere so that I can't talk to her."

Dalton continued to try to smooth out the unfortunate creases inflicted on his new blazer. "Of all the asinine accusations. There isn't a shed of truth to it," he said looking from one to the other of his parents before returning his attention to Connor. "You've lost your mind."

Connor was not to be mollified. "Have I? I saw you two together the other night, but Sarah wouldn't tell me anything other than you drove her home."

"Because that's all that happened," spat Dalton.

Connor was still breathing heavily. "Are you sure about that? What did you say to her to get her to drop me? What lies did you tell?"

Dalton was flushed, his fists balled. "I didn't need to tell her any lies, little brother. There was plenty of truth to go around."

Connor shifted his stance, squaring his shoulders. "I assume you're talking about Gladys."

Dalton was rigid. "Yes, I'm talking about Gladys. Admit it, you've been two-timing your pretty little bride to be and then you come in here and act all sanctimonious when Sarah does the right thing and refuses to marry you because of it."

Connor never took his eyes off his brother. "And who told you about Gladys in the first place?"

Agnes folded her arms. "I did, sweetheart. It's about time you faced the truth and did something about it. Sarah Estey was never right for you. Gladys was the perfect choice all along. I didn't see any reason to hide the fact you decided to go and see her rather than call her on the telephone."

Pritchard stood with his hands on his hips, as though ready to separate the two combatants again if necessary. "Is this true, Connor? Were you seeing the Biddington girl behind your fiancé's back?"

Connor swung his attention to his father. "You make it sound as though we were having an affair. I simply wanted to go and say hello. She's an old friend."

Pritchard regarded his son with a set jaw. "In my day that was called seeing another woman behind your fiancé's back. Why did you do it if there wasn't still something there you wanted to pursue, not that it wouldn't please your mother and me if you did. You know how we feel about it."

Connor swerved away. "I guess I just wanted to see how she was doing. I let her down pretty hard when I met Sarah, and I've always regretted it. Maybe I wanted to make things right while I could. It wouldn't look too good if I waited until after I was married to do so would it? So I was glad she provided me with the opportunity to talk, but I in no way gave her any inclination I was interested in seeing her again. We understand each other and she wished me well. It was nothing more than that, perfectly innocent." He turned his attention back to Dalton. "And then big mouth here couldn't wait to go and turn Sarah against me so he could have her for his own."

Dalton ran his fingers through close-cropped hair. "I felt she had a right to know what you were doing behind her back."

Connor made another lunge for his brother, but Dalton managed to sidestep him before Pritchard could get between them. "You had no right to stick your nose in where it didn't belong, Dalton. And now, because of you, she doesn't want to marry me."

Agnes laid her hand on Connor's arm. "Darling, I know it hurts but it's for the best in the long run. Neither family thought this was a good match from the beginning. Maybe things have just run their natural course and will sort themselves out in the long run."

Connor rounded on his mother. "Sarah and I thought it was a good match, and we were the ones getting married."

Dalton was braver now that his father had separated him from Connor. "I think you believed you could have both Sarah *and* Gladys because that's the way you've always been, Connor ... greedy. You just don't like that it's blown up in your face."

Connor stabbed a forefinger in his brother's direction again. "You just better watch your back, Dalton. This isn't over. You may think you've destroyed my chances with Sarah, but I promise you one thing, I will get her back. She's mine, and she'll always be mine. And what's more I'll find her in time for the wedding. I'll even take her to meet Gladys who'll tell her she has nothing to worry about. So don't put your tuxedo in mothballs just yet, big brother. You'll still be dancing at my wedding, that is if you have the gall to show up."

Dalton rolled his eyes. "That's not going to happen, and you know it. That ship has sailed. If you think there's going to be a wedding now you'd better get on over to Gladys' house and fit her up for a dress,

134

that's if she's still interested in becoming Mrs. Connor McLagen."

Connor gritted his teeth. "You know where Sarah is, don't you? Where did she go, Dalton?"

Dalton looked away. "If you love her so much don't stand here yammering, go and find her ... if you can."

* * *

As the evening wore on Maude's nerves grew worse. She hadn't been able to eat supper, although Cranston had certainly tucked enough away for both of them. She could not fathom how he could remain so indifferent. Sarah was only eighteen and perhaps in need of their help. It didn't ease her mood any when an hour or so later heavy rain that had been forecast for the area began to fall with a vengeance, sluicing against the parsonage windows. Thankfully, though, the storm passed quickly and the sky brightened.

Two more hours dragged by. She glanced at the clock for what must be the hundredth time. It now read nine-fifteen. Maybe Cranston was right, perhaps she was overreacting. She'd been known to do that before. She had to admit she did become unduly anxious about things that others took in stride. Hadn't Cranston been right on more than one occasion in that assessment of his wife? Situations she thought to be dire

135

had resolved themselves nicely just as Cranston predicted they would? But this was different in every way.

She looked at the clock again. Three more minutes gone, and no Sarah coming in the back door full of apologies and explanations. It had now been more than twenty-four hours since she'd last seen her daughter although it felt like much longer.

Cranston was still in his study, working on his sermon she presumed. He did work hard. Everyone said so. He was highly regarded and had received a ringing vote of confidence at the last board of trustees meeting. They'd even given him a raise and allowed him to have a telephone installed for emergency calls. Heretofore someone had to travel to the parsonage, often in the dead of night to fetch him for one thing or another. Many in the village now had telephones anyway and although in this case it was for the pastor, she did make occasional use of it herself.

She looked at the clock again. Nine-twenty. In that moment she made up her mind to call Fanny. She'd talked to her at school this morning, but maybe Fanny assumed Sarah was home by now. Perhaps she might recall something that would put her mind at ease. Maybe Sarah was even at Fanny's house and had asked her friend not to tell. Sarah may have even turned up at school to teach afternoon class for all she knew.

Maude understood it was late to make a personal call and hoped while the Hobson line was ringing that she wasn't getting anyone out of bed.

It was answered on the other end by a man's stern voice. That had to be Fanny's Uncle Frederick and understandably he didn't sound welcoming. She had only spoken to him a few times, and never on a telephone.

"Mr. Hobson?" she asked, aware she sounded timid.

"Yes, this is Frederick Hobson here. Who is speaking please?"

"This is Maude Estey and I'm very sorry to be calling at such a late hour. I was wondering if I might speak to Fanny for a moment. Would she be there by any chance?"

He hesitated for a moment. "Hello, Mrs. Estey. Fanny is right here and she will speak with you."

She breathed a sigh of relief as she heard the phone being passed over with a murmur of who was calling.

"Hello, Mrs. Estey!" came Fanny's over-bright voice. She was larger than life, both in her robust stature and personality. "I'll bet you're calling to tell me that Sarah has come back home, all safe and sound."

"No, Fanny, Sarah has not come home, and I have to tell you I am mightily worried. I want my daughter back here where she belongs. I know we spoke earlier today, but can you give me any more information at all as to where you think she might be?"

Fanny didn't hesitate for a moment. "Hmmm. Well, only what I told you this morning at school. We went into the city yesterday to run some last-minute errands for the wedding and then came home."

"But that's what I find so unusual, Fanny. You said she picked up her shoes at MRA's, so why if she went to all the trouble of doing that would she call off the wedding just hours later? Did she say anything to you about doubts she may have been having?"

"Doubts?"

"I assume she had doubts if she decided not to get married. She must have shared something with you. Any light you can shed on this would be most helpful."

"I don't recall her sharing any doubts with me. If she was having them, she sure didn't say anything about it. We just took care of whatever errands there were to do."

"And then you came back home."

"That's right."

"Fanny, is she perturbed with her father or me?"

Now there *was* a hesitation. "Perturbed?"

"I know very well she knew we were not in favour of who she was marrying, but that wasn't something made known to her at the last minute."

"She did mention she was upset to come home and find that missionary there for dinner."

"Thomas Chaffee."

"That's his name. She felt he was being forced on her and she didn't like him. She said there was something about him that gave her the creeps. She didn't trust him at all. She was scared of him."

"My goodness, that's the first I've heard she felt that way. He wasn't staying here, Fanny, but yes, Sarah's father made it clear he wanted her to marry Thomas and I'm afraid I went along with it. It was wrong of us to do that."

"And since she was already engaged to be married to Connor it made her uncomfortable," Fanny continued. "It frightened her when he followed her down the road. I'm sorry. I know I'm overstepping."

"I'm glad you told me about this, I mean not just that she didn't want to marry him. Fanny, is Sarah there with you now by any chance?"

"Here? Sarah? No, she left shortly after we got home."

"What time was that?"

"About seven I'd say."

"So it would have been daylight."

"Oh yes, and sunny, remember? She said she needed a nice walk home to help her relax."

"But wouldn't she have been carrying parcels?"

"Yes, come to think of it, but only shoes and a couple of other small items so she could manage it all right. But when she saw Connor drive in, she went with him instead. Like a white knight he swooped down and rescued the damsel in distress."

"Damsel in distress?"

"So to speak." Fanny laughed. "She was always calling Connor her white knight, but anyway, he came along at just the right moment and offered to drive her home. She said yes, but I wondered if maybe I shouldn't have driven her home myself."

"Oh? Why is that?"

"Because something was wrong. I didn't want to say anything as it was none of my business. I heard them arguing as they drove off. It sounded like he was really angry with her about something. I heard him yell: "I've had enough," or "that's enough," or something like that. That's all I was able to hear, but you know what they say: The course of true love never did run smooth. I'm sure they had it all worked out by the time he dropped her off, or maybe not."

Chapter Eight

Fanny explained there was nothing more she could tell her. Connor and Sarah were quarrelling and so it should come as no surprise the wedding had been called off.

Maude was in a daze when she hung up, remembering not two hours ago when Connor had come calling for his fiancé, shocked that she wasn't at home. Perhaps he was embarrassed, pretending to be the injured party when all along he knew there was not going to be a wedding.

* * *

An inveterate early riser, Mrs. Wakefield stretched large. Dressing quickly, she pulled her sweater more securely around her slim frame. She'd just spent her first night at her lovely new home she would share with her seafaring husband, Jacob Wakefield. He was expected back in port any day and he'd asked her to wait for him before heading to their new home. He'd thought perhaps she'd be a bit timid to go there by herself, but she was made of sterner stuff than that and assured him she'd be fine. She'd headed up here last night, wanting to do just this. Wake up in her new bed in her new home and do some exploring on her own.

She'd grown up beside the sea in Halifax, the only child of T. Mitchell Holiday, owner of Holiday Steel, the largest company of its kind in North America. He was a very wealthy man, and an indulgent father. That commitment had redoubled following the death of her mother when Stenora was eleven.

This Saint John home that sat not far from the shores of the Bay of Fundy was his wedding gift to Stenora and her husband, a man he had handpicked for his daughter. It had worked out well because she adored the man she'd married six months ago. Given a free hand in the house design, she had met with the architects on more than one occasion to lay out her wishes for what she referred to as the perfect estate. After all, she reasoned, she and Jacob were going to spend the rest of their lives here, raise a whole brood of children now that her husband had agreed this was going to be his last time at sea. A new company had already been set up in his name, so the future looked entirely bright.

Everything had seemed perfect when she'd climbed the driveway last night even in a torrential downpour, although it hadn't lasted long. The grounds were of particular interest to her, designed with her specific taste for roses in mind. Stenora loved roses, lots of them. She'd requested a large rose garden, one laid out with paths and a place to repose with a good book or take a meal. She fancied old-world rose varieties, nothing finicky or fancy, just plants that would fill their days and nights with their summer fragrance.

She was anxious to be in her rose garden, not just see the glistening bushes through the window of her automobile, but unfortunately the inclement weather meant she'd have to wait until morning for a closer look. She'd smiled last night when she'd noticed a rainbow, a portent of the happiness awaiting her here.

And now it was a gorgeous June morning and she breathed in lungfuls of fresh air as she made her way along the cobblestone pathways. The garden was entrancing, and she went to each rosebush in turn: purple, yellow, white, pink, their mingled fragrances intoxicating. She headed for a spacious bench meant for sitting and enjoying the surrounding beauty, a butterfly and honeybee paradise as they sipped the delicious nectar. When she got to the bench she could see it was still puddled with last night's rain. She should have brought a towel.

No worry, she'd just continue visiting each individual bush, dipping her head eagerly to inhale their exquisite perfume. She couldn't wait to clip some of these beauties to take indoors for her breakfast table.

She made a note to herself to find the gardener or gardeners and thank them personally for their superb work. That thought had no sooner passed through her mind than she noticed the far corner of the last rose bed. Perhaps they'd finished in a hurry because the bushes were not properly set at all. Oh my! They were large bushes, most already in bloom, but they hadn't been sunk deep enough into the ground it seemed at first glance. They rode much higher than the others and had already begun to wilt despite the wet soil around them. What on earth!

More curious than annoyed she made her way there, appreciating the large stone sundial had been placed exactly where she'd requested at the end of the walkway. But the rose bushes beyond! Standing with her hands on her hips to assess this unacceptable shoddiness, her heart did a somersault. There, thrust upward among the roses in a shallow grave was a woman's delicate hand.

* * *

Maude laid awake most of the night listening to Cranston snore, plenty of time to make up her mind that she'd somehow convince her husband once and for all they had to look for Sarah. They were now entering day two and something must be done. It was past three the last time she looked at the clock and was still sandy-eyed when the alarm went off at seven.

Cranston seemed in a chipper mood as he dressed in his usual matching jacket, waistcoat, and trousers. His high-collared shirt was also out of date, but this ensemble remained his stubborn preference. He kept his hair neatly trimmed with a centre part, but his mutton-chop sideburns were hopelessly out of fashion.

"I believe I'll have an omelette this morning, Maude. I'm in the mood for something a little lighter than oatmeal. We do have eggs, don't we? I understood Edna Banks was to drop off two dozen fresh eggs on her way to Saint John yesterday."

Maude's appetite was still absent, resentment rushing through her at Cranston's upbeat mood. Why was she the only one suffering? "Yes, Edna brought the eggs and they're in the icebox. Would you like a one-egg omelette or two?"

"Two, as usual. Add a bit of cheese if you have it and don't tarry. I must get to the church early this morning. Some matters can't wait."

She hesitated. "Cranston, about Sarah."

She jumped when he thumped his fist onto the table. "Will you please shut up about that girl? I've had enough of it. She's run off, I tell you. Stop dithering, it's getting on my nerves. I don't know where a man has to go to get some peace and quiet."

Maude burst into tears. There was no way to hold them back, her mood wretched.

"And stop that infernal crying!"

She turned away, stricken as she went to the icebox for the eggs. Within minutes she had an omelette cooking, drying her eyes with the backs of her hands as she did so. Never in her life had she felt so utterly helpless.

When Cranston had finished his breakfast, the entire meal taken in silence, she cleared the dishes and wiped down the table as he slipped into his suit jacket and pulled the door shut with a resounding bang behind him. Never in that moment had she hated him more, although she knew it was a sin to feel the way she did, especially about her husband. The idea of leaving him was as foreign to her as horse feathers, but if ever she was sorely tempted to do so, it would be on a morning like this. No matter, if Sarah was not back by this evening, she was contacting the authorities. Enough was enough. Doing so would likely render her homeless because if Cranston didn't throw her out for defying him, she would in all likelihood seek refuge elsewhere. Life with this impossible man had become unbearable, especially in the last few days. People spoke more kindly to their dogs. She'd heard them.

She thought about the events of last night. Cranston had come home late after taking Thomas Chaffee to Saint John. She'd wakened to find her husband standing by the window, silhouetted in the moonlight. He was deep in thought, obviously unaware Maude was awake and watching him. She could see tears on his cheeks and immediately wondered what was the matter? But something told her she must not interfere in this private moment. Whatever was troubling him was obviously not meant to be shared or he would have already done so. It only served to underline how distant they were as man and wife. They only appeared to be of one mind because she went along with whatever he dictated. Autocratic to the core, it was always his thoughts that directed the marriage, never hers. She was nothing more than a glorified housekeeper. She closed her eyes, embarrassed somehow to be glimpsing this private moment. She did feel a twinge of empathy for him, but it did not stir her heart the way it would have if she loved him. She rued the day she'd ever said *I do* to Reverend Cranston Estey.

* * *

"I won't be going into the office today," Connor announced to his father at the breakfast table that morning. "I've decided to take a few days off."

Agnes glanced furtively at her husband but held her tongue.

Pritchard selected a fresh-baked croissant from the basket in the middle of the table and buttered it with a silver butter knife. He took a generous bite and chewed thoughtfully.

Connor laid down his fork. "I said I won't...."

Pritchard swallowed his mouthful of croissant. "I heard you."

Connor laid his knife on the plate beside his fork. "I'm not sure when I'll be back."

Pritchard reached for his coffee and took a long drink before he finally responded. "You'll do no such thing, Connor. I expect you at the office this morning as usual. It is a busy time with our fiscal year-end nearing, and I can't spare you."

Connor stared at his father. "Under the circumstances...."

Pritchard fixed him with his own steely stare. "Under what circumstances? A cold-footed fiancé who took to the hills rather than marry you? I say good riddance." He held up his hand when he saw Connor was about to sputter his outrage. "Yes, good riddance and I won't pretend otherwise to spare your feelings. You're twenty-four now, Connor. You're a man and I expect you to deal with this in a manly way. Life is full of disappointments. Take this in stride and buck up. Now, you can ride into the city with me or come along on your own if you need a few more minutes, but that is the only leeway I will give you." He got to his feet. "I'll see you later at the office, nine o'clock to be exact."

Pritchard pecked Agnes dutifully on the cheek before stepping out into the bright morning sunshine.

Connor threw down his napkin, glowering.

Agnes dabbed at her lips before folding her napkin, more for something to do it seemed than for any other reason and laid it beside her plate. "Your father is right, Connor. This is a bitter life lesson, but I'm not surprised, choosing from the bottom of the bucket as you did. You choose someone from a lower class, that's the type of behaviour you're bound to expect. Gladys Biddington would never treat you, a McLagen, in such an abominable fashion."

Connor shoved himself away from the table regarding his mother angrily. "This has all worked out very nicely for you and father ... and Dalton, hasn't it!"

"Oh, stop being dramatic, darling. Water has a way of rising to its own level in matters such as these. I guarantee one day you'll look at this day and chuckle, and how you almost made the mistake of marrying the wrong woman. Now do as your father has told you and head into the office. Come on, darling, there'll be harder things than this to get through in life. You'll be surprised I'm sure how quickly you bounce back. You're young. You've got your whole life ahead of you. And you have a lovely young woman down the road, a cherished family friend, who is just waiting to be asked. I can't see what the downside is really."

He barely nodded as he went around the table and headed for the hall.

"Connor," said his mother as he walked past, "what happened to your hand? I never noticed 'til now, but it's quite swollen and scratched."

* * *

Dalton dispatched the papers off the desk angrily with the sweep of his arm. He was in no mood to work on the Coker New Brunswick file today. Normally he liked tedious work, he was at his best doing research although he was expected to gain experience in the courtroom as well. The bad with the good. It was all in a day's work he knew. He loved law, knew he'd chosen the right career, but today he wished he were anywhere but here.

The events of the past few days had unnerved him. Why couldn't he have left well enough alone? But there was something about Sarah that simultaneously drew him to her like a moth to flame, but also infuriated him beyond reason. He could have any woman he wanted, that had been made patently clear on any number of occasions. Perhaps it was a case of wanting something he couldn't have, would never have now apparently. Whatever it was it had gotten under his skin like the seven-year itch.

Sarah was an elusive trophy, one that he hungered for. She'd dropped him like a hot potato for his younger brother, but he'd always assumed she'd eventually regret that. Connor had his good points, it was true, but could not offer her the same things he could. Being older he was more worldly, more experienced. And how fetching she would look on his arm. True she could not help him socially, but her beauty provided more than enough counterbalance. That he had been denied her, that she'd treated him like some common errand boy still galled him. How dare she!

He balled his hands into fists at the thought of it, his own strength surprising him.

* * *

Pritchard made his way down King Street, the calm waters of Saint John Harbour flung before him like a blue crystal jewel, boats resting at dockside in Market Slip at high tide. Waiting nearby were teams of horses standing side by side hitched to sloven wagons or express wagons, the teamsters mingling for a little early-morning conversation as they waited in line to be hired. It seemed everyone's mood was light today, the pot of gold after last evening's downpour that had scrubbed everything clean then finished the job with a rainbow. He thought about the events of the past twenty-four hours, and before that if he considered the entire picture. He would be forever grateful the situation with Connor's fiancé had been taken care of. No matter where she was at the moment, she would no longer be a thorn in his side with those Prohibitionist parents of hers. It was a question of time before they made trouble for him if only by innuendo. There had certainly been rumblings of it despite the fact that Prohibition would soon be over.

Connor was his favoured son. He would make no apologies for that, but he had missed the mark entirely when he'd picked Sarah. The ending had been messy, that was just collateral damage. One thing was for certain, he would bring all his weight to bear when it came time for Connor to choose a new bride. He and Agnes would champion Gladys Biddington, make it impossible for him to refuse her.

He was in deep thought as he left his automobile in its usual parking spot and began to cover the short distance to his office. It was inescapable, there had to be a storm before there could be a rainbow, and now the storm was over and so were their problems.

As he settled at his desk minutes later, he folded his hands in front of him on the polished mahogany, watching the sun perform its tantalizing dance across the water. He, not Connor, had lost a pretty penny on all the wedding preparations, but he did not consider it wasted money. When you weighed out the cost of a few fripperies against what he would have lost with Cranston Estey pounding the pulpit about McLagen business affairs, it was inconsequential. Things would ease now that Prohibition had been repealed, but he owed Cranston for the trouble he'd made for him in the past. If he never heard the name Estey again in his life, it would be too soon.

* * *

Maude sat on the edge of Sarah's bed, her daughter's wedding dress laid out beside her. Mabel Walker had delivered it earlier, the dressmaker unaware of the change of plans. Maude ran her fingers over the exquisite creation, the cool silk whispering under the gentle touch of her fingers. She thought of her own wedding. It was as utilitarian as they came. She'd made her own dress out of white muslin and while she supposed it was as acceptable as any other bridal gown in 1890, the ridiculous feathered hat she'd thought was a good idea at the time, was not. There was a wedding photograph of the unlikely looking couple tucked away somewhere in the house, and that's just where it could stay. Tucked away. She didn't need to dig it out to remember how stern Cranston had looked, as though he was waiting to have a tooth extracted. Now that she thought about it, that's what these past thirty-seven years had been like, one big tooth extraction.

She thought of the day the tiny golden-haired bundle had been passed to her, and she became a mother. Cranston never held the child or made of her in any way, obviously feeling that providing food and shelter was an adequate commitment. He'd done his duty by taking the baby in.

She'd dreamed of having a child of her own but after their initial clumsy attempt at lovemaking, she was just as happy to have one given to her rather than go through the agony of *that* exchange on anything like a regular basis.

She wondered what her life would have been like if she'd been able to choose her own husband, not that she'd been inundated with young men asking for her hand. There had been a young man at church though, handsome but for a rather pronounced overbite, and she had been attracted to him. He too was interested but her mother had seen what was happening and stepped in, promising her daughter to the more desirable bachelor, Reverend Cranston Estey and her father had not intervened. Several women had set their cap for Cranston, and now, all these years later, her only regret was that she'd been the successful spinster. If the others only knew what they'd been spared!

'And then I turned around and tried to do the same thing with my own daughter,' she wept aloud. Helping Cranston to promote Thomas Chaffee amounted to the same thing. She suddenly admired Sarah for standing up to them. If only she'd had half the courage her daughter had. Sarah took a back seat to no one, and where once she'd felt threatened by that, even as recently as two days ago, she now admired her gumption. When she came back home things would be much different between them. If only she had the chance to correct some of the mistakes she'd made in raising her daughter, she'd waste no time getting it done. She was already planning in her head the mother/daughter talk they would have together. She'd tell her if she wanted to marry Connor McLagen, if she was in love with him and thought he could make her happy, she'd give her heartfelt blessing. Yes, she would finally make a lot of things right.

She would stand up to Cranston, speak up on Sarah's behalf. She'd read somewhere that calmness and courage could both be learned, and it was something to think about. Could she change? Other people had. She could feel something growing in her, sprouting from a tiny seed and coming to life. Had this realization come too late?

She couldn't think like that. Perhaps Sarah was punishing them for being so difficult, it wasn't like she didn't have good cause.

"Oh, Sarah," she wailed aloud on a fresh set of tears, "where are you? Please come home. Things are going to be so different."

* * *

Gladys picked up her flower basket and headed into the garden, thinking about the gossip that had already taken on a life of its own. So, Sarah had called off the wedding. That meant Connor was wonderfully free. Sure, he'd be down for a while, broken-hearted if she knew Connor. Once he'd healed, she'd do her best to get him back. She should have fought harder to keep him at the time, but she'd been as shocked as the next person when he had unexpectedly ended their relationship. She'd received an invitation to that gathering last year where he'd met Sarah but had begged off because of a headache. If she had that particular evening to live over again, she would certainly do things much differently. She'd missed it and lost her beau.

She'd always assumed she and Connor would be married, as had both families, but she'd had to stand in the shadows while Connor and Sarah's love affair blossomed.

Now Sarah was out of the way. Gladys smiled as she cut a bouquet of fresh roses from the garden for the dining room table. There was just something about roses.

* * *

Thomas Chaffee poured himself a cup of coffee then immediately pushed it away, bereft. He'd gone to Reverend Estey last night at what was likely the worst time in his life, and Cranston had helped him. The reverend was not only a mentor but had proven to be a very good friend.

He dropped his head into his hands. He'd so been looking forward to his furlough, a rest from his demanding work in The Belgian Congo. He loved what he did, certainly, but he was exhausted. A lot was asked of him, and he had given generously of himself until it didn't seem as though there was much more to give. And now he had no alternative but to leave town quickly because he knew the terrible consequences if he stayed and faced the music. He was a much different man than he'd been just two days ago. Now he loathed himself.

Reverend Estey was making arrangements for him to return to the African continent immediately where he'd hopefully be safely out of reach. And what other alternative did he have but to remain there indefinitely? But no matter where he was, he knew he had to live with himself for the rest of his life. A tidal wave of angst swept over him as he fell to his knees sobbing.

"Father," he implored in tearful prayer, "please, I beg you. Forgive me for what I have done."

Chapter Nine

Following breakfast the next morning, Maude watched Cranston through the hall window as he unlocked the back door to the church and disappeared inside. He was a man of fastidious habit and unless something pulled him away from matters awaiting him there, she wouldn't see him again until noontime ... well, 12:30. Perfect, because she had decided to call the police about Sarah.

Her hands were moist as she carefully dialled the number and it seemed she waited on the line for an eternity until she heard a man's voice identify himself as Constable Harrington. After telling him who was calling, she quickly explained how her daughter had not come home night before last. That Sarah was a teacher and this behaviour was uncharacteristic of her responsible nature. And that was as far as she got, cut off in mid-sentence.

"How old is she?" he asked abruptly.

"Eighteen."

The constable did not sound like a young man, but it was clear from his tone of voice he'd heard enough. "She's just run off. She's got her first taste of freedom and she's making the most of it. I wouldn't worry too much."

"But I *am* worried."

He chuckled and even that sounded condescending. "I wouldn't be. You know girls these days ... modern women they call themselves. Give her a few more days and she'll be back."

"But she was to be married tomorrow."

"Ahh, there you have it. Cold feet, we've seen this type of thing before. She'll turn up full of apologies in a day or so."

Maude felt like screaming. Why did no one take this seriously? "Constable, I'm frightened. I really do think something has happened to her. This is not like her at all."

"Can I speak to the girl's father please?" he asked, exhaling impatiently.

"He's not home at the moment."

"What does he say about your daughter being away?"

She was reluctant to answer that question, but she was after all talking to the police, asking for their help. She must be honest even though she pretty much knew how he'd respond.

"My husband believes she'll be back in a day or so."

"There you go! Look, Madam, your daughter wouldn't be the first to change her mind and run off. Make sure to leave the porch light on. There's no question in my mind she'll be back. She's a teenager and teenagers do silly things. Have a good stern talk to her when she does get home. Good day now," and with that she was dismissed.

She resisted the urge to slam down the receiver in exasperation but only because she'd have to account for a broken telephone. She settled instead for a short prayer to calm her nerves and it seemed to work because by noon she was at least able to tolerate Cranston.

She played the dutiful wife when he came home for lunch, serving him soup and a roll without comment. He lingered over tea, enjoying one of her strawberry jam tarts as he would on any other day, but it was obvious today he preferred silence. Fine. She served that up too in generous helpings. When he'd finished, he rose from the table, dabbed at the corners of his mouth with a napkin, slipped on his suit jacket and left by the back door heading for the church where his black Model T was parked. Friday afternoons were set aside for sick and shut-in visitation. She continued to watch as he fired the automobile to life and made his way onto the main road at a turtle's pace. Only then did she breathe a sigh of relief.

Not more than five words had passed between them since early this morning and Sarah's name had not been one of them. It didn't matter now anyway because she hadn't been able to get any traction at all with the police. It had felt good though to take matters into her own hands instead of always waiting for Cranston to assume the lead. If she'd gotten results, it would be worth what she'd have to put up with when her husband found out what she'd done without his permission, or more accurately, specifically against his wishes.

* * *

Stenora sipped her coffee, hot and strong, working to steady her nerves following the grisly discovery she'd made in her new rose garden. Still reeling from what she'd found, she'd been galvanized into action, summoning the police immediately. They had arrived in numbers and soon her lovely rose garden with its soggy lawns had been churned into a soupy mess by countless footsteps.

It hadn't taken police long to fully unearth the body, that of a very small blonde woman, but how she'd gotten into Stenora Wakefield's rose garden was a complete mystery. And because the body had been found on the family property she was the first person to be questioned, extensively, but she was as much in the dark as everyone else.

The landscaper and the gardener were the next to be put on the hot seat once they'd been rounded up, the gardener still recovering from a bad bout of bronchitis. She didn't even want to think that her father, who had overseen all facets of this property development for his daughter and son-in-law, had unwittingly hired murderers to do the job. The worst of it was she had an idea the officers didn't believe what she was telling them, that she had absolutely no idea what was going on. Suspicion was written all over their faces when she told them she had come to her new home the night before and happened to stumble across the body this morning. It sounded as ridiculous to her own ears as she knew it sounded to theirs. She hadn't a clue as to who the young woman was or where she'd come from, and her interrogators eventually decided she was telling the truth.

Meanwhile an autopsy was being conducted on the remains.

* * *

"Extra! Extra! Read all about it. Mystery woman found murdered!" shouted the newsboy at the head of the Saint John City Market on Charlotte Street: YOUNG, BEAUTIFUL AND DEAD, was the stuff of headlines and business was brisk. "Get your copy right here!" he sang out.

Dalton could hear the newsboy's call from his usual spot across the street from the law office, and he looked out to see passersby eagerly purchasing their copy, many stopping where they stood to read the day's top story. It was probably some poor drunken wretch, Dalton thought as he watched the spectacle. Well, it served her right if that was the case. Some people never do an honest day's work in their lives, and they turn up dead somewhere. Then there's a big hullabaloo. He got up to close the window. He had enough on his mind without listening to someone else's troubles. They'd likely never identify her anyway, isn't that the way these things usually went? No one would report her missing, or care that she was dead.

Returning to his work he continued to peruse case law in the New Brunswick Statutes, searching for a judge's written decision, a precedent that would most closely parallel the file he was working on. So far, no luck because what he needed to find was proving to be as elusive as his peace of mind.

* * *

Maude was still upset about her poor luck with the constable this morning. She was sure he'd only heard the ranting of an overwrought housewife and when she'd told him her husband agreed with what he was saying it had played right into his hands. It might be the day of the modern woman, but what *this* woman said hadn't carried any weight at all. That much was obvious, and she felt the frustration keenly. Cranston refused to discuss it and the police weren't interested. Where was she supposed to start looking?

She'd made bread this afternoon, to keep occupied. Otherwise, she would go out of her mind with worry. She was lifting the loaves out of the oven when Cranston walked in the back door and laid the evening paper on the table beside a vase of wilted lilacs.

"That bread smells good, Maude," he told her without glancing in her direction. "It's about time you made some fresh. I hope you have supper started, I'm hungry."

She reached down deep inside to find it within herself to speak to him. "Supper will be ready at five, as usual," she told him not bothering to soften the edge in her voice with an apology as she would normally do.

"No need to be testy," he admonished as he picked up the newspaper and opened it.

Maude saw the banner headline and felt the room begin to spin. She went off balance, nearly falling and it was a few moments before the room righted itself. Still not trusting her legs for support she held onto the door casing.

"It's her! I know it is!" she shrieked.

"Maude! Stop getting yourself all upset. It's likely some other woman, someone from the streets. Saint John is a port city, there are people coming and going all the time. A good deal of the population is unsavoury. You go flopping about the place as though you know it's her. Why do you expect Sarah to be dead?"

Now recovered, she snatched the paper from his hand, tearing it badly as he tried to prevent her from taking it. "Look right here," she said through tears. "She is described as tiny, light blonde hair and blue eyes; wearing a beige dress with white trim and white suede shoes. Cranston! That describes Sarah to a tee! Oh no no no no!" she wailed. "Nooooo!"

He grabbed the torn newspaper back from his wife. "Maude! Settle down for heavens sake! Just because it sounds like her doesn't mean it is for certain. Give it time I tell you!"

Maude started for the telephone. "I'm calling the police. That is our daughter! I know it and you know it. If you had any sense, you would stop denying anything is wrong and help me. Help me, Cranston! Do something!"

"We'll look like fools if we go off in all directions," he sputtered. "I have my reputation as the reverend of the second largest church in this area to think of. We will have to wait until we know for certain it's actually her. And God forbid if that's the case because it will mean a terrible scandal."

Maude shrieked even louder, Cranston's eyes widening at his normally placid wife's recalcitrant behaviour. "I simply cannot bear you anymore, Cranston Estey! Everything is about you, always has been. We could have been looking for her two days ago and we might have prevented something like this happening. But *no*, you said! Be still, Maude! Don't get yourself so worked up, Maude! I knew she needed help, and you wouldn't lift a finger. You're a disgrace as a father and a husband!"

She saw the blow coming, but not in enough time to avoid it and the backhand knocked her to her knees. But instead of cowering she got slowly to her feet, tasting blood as she went to the telephone. "You'll have to kill me, Cranston, if you want to stop me. One would think you'd want to be the one making the call, you being such a reputable reverend and all."

His hands dropped to his side. "I'm sorry, Maude. This whole thing has taken its toll on me too. I'll make the call, get out of the way."

* * *

It seemed like an interminable length of time before the police arrived, two detectives knocking at the back door before Maude ushered them inside. The older, stocky man introduced himself as Peter Halverson. The other man, a half a head taller was Frank London. Maude showed them into the living room, the hanky she held to her eyes already drenched with tears. For his part Cranston sat with a set jaw, dry-eyed, staring straight ahead. She'd had time to ice the swelling on her cheek from Cranston's right hand and to her estimation it looked fine. Besides, her face was already swollen from crying. What did it matter anyway?

The first thing they asked for was a picture of Sarah, and they nodded quietly as they identified her as the body found buried in the rose garden. Once that preliminary matter was taken care of, Halverson took out a well-worn notebook and pencil in readiness for the information he hoped to glean from the parents. There were the usual questions to be got through: Did Sarah have any enemies? Did they have any idea who would do such a thing? What was their relationship like with her? Had there been a family quarrel of any kind, and the like. All the while the two detectives observed them.

Maude continued to dab at her eyes. "May I ask how she died?"

London leaned forward, his elbows on his knees. "We're not at liberty to reveal the autopsy findings."

Cranston finally spoke, his voice sounding hoarse and painful. "She was wearing an expensive diamond ring. Has that been accounted for may I ask?"

London shook his head. "There was no jewellery found on the victim. Are you certain she would have been wearing it?"

Cranston didn't seem to be speaking to anyone in particular, his gaze fixed on the far side of the room. "I don't see what reason there'd be to take it off."

Maude wiped her eyes and nose. "She may not have been wearing it. I found a note in her room saying she'd changed her mind about getting married. Tomorrow was to be her wedding day. She said she was leaving town and asked that we not look for her."

Interest flared in the eyes of both detectives. "Do you still have that note?" London asked Maude.

Her voice was barely above a whisper. "Yes I do," she said producing it and apologizing that it was a bit wrinkled. That wasn't surprising considering how many times she'd read it, held it, cried over it.

They both read it. "Is this your daughter's handwriting?"

Maude began to speak but Cranston overrode her. "Of course it's Sarah's handwriting. Who else do you suppose might have written it? She changed her mind and went off, foolishly. As dreadful as that is I don't see why you have to come here and imply we had anything to do with it."

Neither detective was fazed by Cranston's rudeness, London responding. "*Did* you have anything to do with your daughter's disappearance and death, Mr. Estey?"

Cranston was absolutely florid. "Of all the absurd things to ask me! We loved our daughter and we had nothing to do with any of this. We're as shocked as everyone else."

Unperturbed London continued as though there'd been no outburst. "It's perfectly normal to speak with you both as

Sarah's parents. We're investigating a murder, Mr. Estey."

Cranston's colour had not improved any in the past several seconds. "It's Reverend Estey."

London nodded. "Sorry, Reverend Estey. As I say we're investigating a murder and we can leave no stone unturned. Having us ask you certain questions may be unpleasant, but I can assure you it's necessary. We don't mean to offend you."

Cranston was not about to be mollified. "Well, we are offended. We've only just found out she's deceased before we're practically accused of her murder. You asked if we might know who would do something like this to Sarah. I suggest you stop wasting your time here and go and see the McLagens. They're back the way you came, going toward town. It's the large grey and white mansion sitting behind a cedar hedge. They call the place Orchard Hill."

Halverson was still busy making notes. "Orchard Hill?"

Cranston turned his attention to Halverson. "Orchard Hill, you'll see apple trees in back. It used to be a farm before the *grand manor* was built by old Horace McLagen about sixty years ago. He was as crooked as a ram's horn too they say. Anyway, talk to Connor McLagen, he's the one Sarah was going to marry. He was probably none too happy she'd finally seen the light and called it off. We were dead set against her marrying into that family. That old man is nothing but a crook, flouting the law as it suits him. Like father, like son."

Halverson looked up. "Would that be the same McLagens as McLagen & Son Ltd. at Market Slip in Saint John?"

Cranston allowed himself a shadow of a smile. "I should think law enforcement would be very well acquainted with *that* firm, because of who's been paid off for protection that is."

London's eyes narrowed. "I beg your pardon?"

It was as though Cranston knew he had gone too far and began to reel himself in. "I suppose every barrel has a rotten apple. I was referring to provincial prohibition inspectors, I certainly didn't mean to imply everyone is dishonest."

London gave Cranston a long, hard look before getting to his feet and turning to Maude. "Will you please take us to Sarah's room? We'd like to have a look in there."

Maude tried to stifle a sob. "Certainly, please follow me."

Once both detectives were in the room, they thanked her before closing the door. Some time later they emerged and headed back to the living room where she and Cranston were waiting.

Maude got nervously to her feet when the detectives returned. "There is something I forgot to tell you. Sarah's best friend is Fanny Hobson. I talked to Fanny to see if she'd seen Sarah since they returned from the city night before last. They'd gone there to attend to a few last-minute errands. She told me Connor had come along after they got back, and Sarah went off with him. She said she heard them arguing before they drove away. I'm sorry, that slipped my mind. That was the night Sarah went missing, although she must have left the note earlier. I didn't notice it until I cleaned the next morning. This is so overwhelming," she finished on a fresh wave of tears.

Halverson made note of Fanny's telephone number. "I understand, but it's good you remembered it now. We'll certainly follow up on that. Thank you for your time, Mr. and Mrs. Estey. We'll be in touch."

Cranston watched them leave the yard and head for the main road. "Infuriating swine! How dare they suggest we had anything to do with this! I despise Sarah in this moment for raining all of this down upon us."

"Sarah is dead, Cranston!" she shouted at him, uncaring it could earn her another backhand. "Have you no feelings at all? Is your heart really so hard toward her?"

He glowered at her. "I'll tell you one thing, I'm not surprised she went and did this to herself."

Maude stared at him. "Did this to herself? How can you say such a thing?"

"When she ran off, she just as well did this to herself is what I mean. I obviously don't think she buried herself you nitwit!"

She had never felt such rage toward the man standing in front of her. "Don't you ever for a moment consider stepping down off your pedestal? The almighty Reverend Estey who beats his wife and hates his child."

"Sarah is exactly like her mother! No good! And you, my good wife, are nothing but a fool! A ... a ... yoke around my neck!"

"And I repeat, you're a disgrace!"

He took an ominous step forward, one forefinger inches from her face. "Not another word, Maude. We have this to get through and we will maintain our dignity as we do. I'm sure you can't imagine the firestorm that's been stirred up. When everything has been got through, I want you to leave this house and never come back. I will say the grief was too much for you."

"I guess it's not too much for you though is it, Cranston?" she asked dangerously. "And you can work out whatever story you want to, I will gladly leave this house and it will probably be before everything has been *got through*."

With that she spun on her heel and left the room heading for the spare room at the back of the house. She didn't feel she should sleep in Sarah's bed, although it would have made her feel closer to her daughter because her scent might still linger. Since this was an active police investigation she knew it would likely be a bad idea to spend the night there.

Once in the guest room she turned the lock on the door, feeling somewhat safer after she did so. Nevertheless, given Cranston's size and temper that lock would only slow him down if he had a mind to enter. She didn't bother to undress, and eventually cried herself to sleep sometime after midnight.

* * *

Pritchard McLagen was on his way back to his office following a meeting on Charlotte Street when he passed the newsboy at the head of the market. He flipped the boy a coin and seized the newspaper, not bothering to unfold it as he continued along Charlotte Street and turned the corner onto King. It was an ideal day as his father used to say, although he'd never said what it was ideal for. Making money, likely.

He raised his hand in greeting to familiar faces as he made his way down the sidewalk to the tune of Constable Duffy's traffic whistle. He glanced at a streetcar climbing the steep hill, sharing the street with horse-drawn delivery wagons. As he approached MRA's, the sprawling emporium with its forty-five departments, he was reminded of his upcoming wedding anniversary. Surely, he'd find something in that grand department store to give his beloved Agnes. Their wedding had been a highlight on the Rothesay social calendar thirty years ago, Agnes a vision in Chantilly lace. She'd given him two healthy sons, and both were prospering. Connor was his favourite, Agnes's too if the truth be told, and he made no apologies for that. He and Dalton were too much alike and so they were prone to locking horns, one just as stubborn as the other.

He glanced in one of MRA's store windows as he passed. He'd have to give it some serious thought as to the perfect gift for his wife. He usually gave her roses but perhaps their thirtieth called for something extra special. Jewellery was probably the best. Diamond cocktail rings were still very popular, and it would be a lovely addition to her substantial jewellery collection.

He thought of Connor again. His youngest son had been on his mind all day. He hadn't spoken with him since this morning, but then again, he'd been tied up in a meeting for the past few hours. He'd look in on him when he got back to the office, but first he wanted to read this sensational news story everyone was talking about. A murder always got people stirred up. She probably came from one of the bawdy houses in town. That's the type of thing one could expect from that crowd.

"You're back, Mr. McLagen," announced his secretary, Mildred McDaniel, unnecessarily when he walked through the glass-panelled door. "Would you like your usual cup of afternoon tea?"

"Yes, please, Mildred. Bring it in when it's steeped."

She smiled, a middle-aged woman who clearly adored her boss. "I have it steeped already because you rarely say no. I'll bring the tray right along."

He didn't wait for the tea before he began to read the lead story. My goodness, this woman was found in a rose garden of all places, on the grounds of a newly constructed mansion on the east side. He read with interest the description of the dead woman, and that she was dressed in linen and wore suede shoes. That didn't sound at all like a flophouse floozy. It was most peculiar, but not surprising. Murders were not an uncommon occurrence in any city. One just had to be careful was all.

Once he'd finished his tea he went to Connor's office, catching him as he was slipping into his blazer. He noticed a copy of a newspaper in his wastepaper basket.

"Leaving early today, son?"

Connor was flushed. "Yes, Father, I can't seem to concentrate." He pointed to his cluttered desk. "I've read those reports a dozen times and the figures just won't stick in my head. I need a few days to myself. I have to get away from everything, have a change of scenery."

Pritchard sighed. "Maybe you're right," he said nodding his head in agreement. "I've been thinking perhaps I was a bit rough on you this morning. You would have been gone for a few weeks on your honeymoon anyway, so it's not like we wouldn't have to be getting along without you. If that's what you need to put this whole thing behind you once and for all, then go ahead. I'll ask Carl to pick up your slack. Take a few days, a week or two even. You can get an early start in the morning for wherever it is you intend to go."

Connor did not meet his father's eyes. "Thank you, Father, but I want to leave now, just as I am. To be honest, my mind is in such a state I think I'll go as the spirit moves me. Don't worry though, I'll call home soon to let you know where I am."

* * *

Cranston waited until Maude had retired before making his call to pass along the required information.

Thomas answered on the first ring and listened intently before speaking. "I want to thank you, Reverend Estey for arranging my transportation at the last minute as you have," he said with emotion once Cranston was finished. "I'm also grateful you were able to convince the Board I wanted to leave right away."

"No need to thank me, Thomas. Your ticket will be waiting for you onboard. I wish you a safe trip back to Africa."

Chapter Ten

Connor's mind was a whirlwind of thoughts when he left the office, still thinking about his visit to Sarah's house the night before, flowers in hand. How had he and his fiancé gotten so off-track things would end the way they did? They had gone off-track the night she'd made the confession she was sexually experienced. It had been an enormous disappointment. He could still feel the letdown of that moment when he realized his beautiful angel wasn't an angel after all.

Sarah sensed things had changed between them. He knew she had, and try as he might not to, he did look at her differently. Maybe that's why Gladys' appeal had suddenly returned. Good ole, faithful Gladdy.

At the moment though he didn't want to be around any woman, no matter how tempting she might be. What was best for him was what he was doing right now, hitting the road to nowhere ... anywhere ... to collect himself, away from everything until he could decide what to do next. Maybe he could even get some sleep, or try to, because he hadn't been able to do so at all over the past couple of nights. His mother, though he adored her, liked to ask questions and offer help when all he wanted was for her to be quiet. Please be quiet, Mother! How could he even begin to come to grips with Sarah's death? The way she'd died?

Nausea curled in his stomach. If anyone had told him his relationship with the beautiful Sarah Estey would end this way, he would have laughed in their face. He felt like screaming, crying, but mostly he trembled, not knowing which direction to turn next. He'd always prided himself on being coolheaded, unflappable. He didn't feel in the least bit coolheaded now, and he definitely wasn't unflappable.

Once behind the wheel he decided to hit the open road. He found himself driving past stately homes on Douglas Avenue crossing over the Reversing Falls Bridge into Lancaster; heading down Manawagonish Road and out onto the road toward St. Stephen. He did not intend to go all the way to that border town. He hadn't even intended to go in this direction at all, but he'd keep driving until he felt like turning around and heading back. He knew it was impossible to outrun Sarah.

He hadn't gone far when he saw a young woman walking along the shoulder of the narrow road. When he stopped beside her, he could see she was actually in her early thirties not to mention a little rough around the edges.

"Can I offer you a lift?" he asked politely, because he felt he shouldn't leave a woman alone on this deserted stretch of road.

She looked at him, prettier when she finally smiled. "Where are you headed?"

Connor shrugged. "Wherever you need to go I guess."

"I'm going to Boston," she announced with a defiant tilt of her chin. "I thought if I was walking on this road someone would come along sooner or later who was headed to the border. Are you going to take me to Boston?"

He hadn't expected her to say that. He'd thought maybe she was going to one of the small fishing villages along the shore. He certainly wouldn't have minded taking her there.

"Sorry, I'm not going quite that far," he apologized. "Are you sure you want to go to Boston?"

She looked him over boldly and judging by her expression she liked what she saw. "Maybe I should say I'm going wherever you're going. You look like you could use some female company."

He thought about that. Before he'd come upon her, he'd thought he wanted to be alone, but she had a willing look to her and so maybe she was right after all. Maybe he did need some company.

He studied her for a moment longer. The more he looked at her the more attractive she became, although her eyes were hard, knowing. No matter, he wasn't going to marry her.

"What's your name?" he asked as he continued to scrutinize her.

She held his gaze without effort. "I'm Maggie Strong," she said, reaching through the car window to shake his hand.

"Well, Maggie, would you like to come with me?"

"For how long?"

"Not for a long time," he told her honestly. "Maybe just for tonight."

"That's fine," she nodded, still smiling. "I do have to get to Boston, but it looks like I'm going to take a little detour. Where are we headed?"

"Back the way I came. Come on, get in."

* * *

The McLagens had retired to the living room for an evening beverage when a knock came to the front door and Pritchard roused himself from his favourite chair to answer it. He was surprised to see two men standing on his doorstep and he reluctantly asked them to come in once they had identified themselves.

Pritchard was doing his best to appear unaffected, but in truth he was outraged to have the police come to his home ... for any reason. It didn't look good. In that moment he connected the dead woman in the newspaper with Sarah Estey. Connor's fiancé had been murdered. That's why the police were here. They suspected Connor. Bells began to go off in his head when he recalled Connor's eagerness to take to his heels. Dear God! That's what Connor got for associating with those Esteys. They would be the ruin of him. A preacher Cranston Estey might be, but they were still trouble to him.

Pritchard tried to keep his expression neutral. "We were relaxing after dinner. May I ask if you gentlemen would care to join us?" he asked, stalling before having to face the inevitable.

Detective London lifted his chin as though he saw right through Pritchard McLagen's affectation. "This isn't a social call, Mr. McLagen. We're here to see Connor McLagen as part of our investigation into the death of Sarah Estey."

The forced smile faded from Pritchard's face. "I read about that in the newspaper. Terrible! What on earth would Connor have to do with that?"

Detective Halverson rocked back on his heels. "We're following all leads."

Agnes McLagen was on her feet, eyes blazing. "This is absurd! If that Estey girl is dead, I can tell you with every certainty my son had nothing to do with it. You have absolutely no right to come barging in here. We are a reputable family."

London appeared unimpressed with Agnes' performance. "Ma'am, as I say we are investigating Sarah Estey's murder. We have to ask...."

Agnes was not to be put off. "And I asked you what on earth Connor would have to do with that? He was her fiancé, that is correct, but he told us she changed her mind about the wedding and left town. And I say good riddance. Connor is still recovering from what she did to him, breaking their engagement the way she did. And now ... this."

Pritchard McLagen was as puffed up as a rooster. "My wife is correct. You have no right to even assume a McLagen is involved in anything of this nature. Isn't it enough she left him at the last minute and ran off? He didn't do anything to that girl, she did it to herself."

A knowing look passed between the two investigators, but they made no comment. A woman could hardly bury herself.

London squared his shoulders. "Could we please speak with Connor?"

Pritchard didn't budge an inch. "He isn't here."

London easily held the angry man's stare. "Where is he?"

Agnes slammed her hands onto her hips. "We don't know where he is and even if we did, we wouldn't tell you because it's none of your business. He's done nothing wrong. He doesn't have to account for his whereabouts like some common criminal."

London's stare had been known to weaken the knees of most men, those who had cause to worry. He directed it now at Pritchard. "This will not go well if you refuse to cooperate or obstruct us in the performance of our duties. We believe Connor was the last person to see Sarah Estey alive and that makes us very interested. We need to talk to him, and we *will* find him. It would be in your best interests to either tell us where he is or tell *him* we want to talk to him. Is he driving or on foot?"

Pritchard clenched his fists. "Driving."

Halverson had his notebook out and ready. "What is he driving and what is the license number please? And I would advise you to give me the correct plate number."

Pritchard recited the make, model, and license plate number although it looked as though it would cost him his last ounce of restraint to do so.

London looked around the room. "Could we please see a picture of your son?"

Agnes bristled. "Why?"

London shifted his attention to her. "Because we want to see what he looks like," he told her, his gaze never wavering.

She walked stiffly to the other side of the room and returned with a framed portrait taken not six months ago. She held it up for both officers to see but did not pass it to them.

London lifted his eyes. "We'd like to take this with us, Ma'am."

Agnes pulled it back, holding onto it as though it was made of solid gold. "Certainly not. This is a family portrait."

Halverson watched her. "Then maybe another one if you have it."

Pritchard nodded at her to cooperate although he looked far from pleased to be doing so. "Give it to him, Agnes, out of the frame," he added pointedly. "We'll get it back once this whole misunderstanding has been cleared up. If they manage to damage or lose it," he said, again eyeing them balefully, "I can easily get another from the photographer. He has the original plates, but the bill for the work will be sent to the Saint John Police Department."

Agnes was a bright shade of pink as she extracted the image from the frame and shoved it in their direction, Halverson removing it with an effort from her unyielding grasp.

London studied it again. "How tall would you say he is, Ma'am? Six feet or so?"

Her lips were as tight as bowstrings. "Exactly six feet," she managed before returning the empty frame to its spot on the side table.

Halverson slipped his notebook and pencil back into his breast pocket. "If we don't find him first, tell him to come to our office in Saint John. He would be very wise to do so as soon as possible."

Pritchard was a pale shade of purple, his colour escalating. "What, so he can be railroaded into confessing to something he didn't do? It would look very good for you to solve this crime quickly, wouldn't it? A real feather in your cap, maybe even a promotion, but I won't allow you to use my son to accomplish that."

Just then Dalton walked into the room. "What's going on? I could hear raised voices all the way out back."

Agnes glared at the two detectives before returning her gaze to her son. "These men are here from the police, and they want to question Connor with respect to that Estey girl's death."

Dalton shrugged. "So, let them question him, get it over with. Why not?"

Pritchard's colour ramped up another notch. "Because Connor is not here at the moment and besides, I should think you as the lawyer of the family would suggest he not do that."

Dalton raised his eyebrows. "What, cooperate with the police? If he's got nothing to hide, what's the problem?"

Pritchard could barely contain his anger at his older son's infuriating nonchalance where the family's good name was concerned. "Because innocent people, especially a McLagen, do not have to answer to such nonsense."

Dalton smirked. "Ahh, but not even us McLagens are above the law, Father. Where is Connor anyway? He's usually home from the office by now. Is he up in his room crying into his pillow because he couldn't have what he wanted?"

London and Halverson again exchanged a meaningful glance.

It would be hard to judge who was the angrier, Pritchard or Agnes, although it was the latter who used her rapier sharp tongue as a weapon. "Dalton, I will demand that you keep a civil tongue in your head and while you're at it, remember you are a McLagen. You are to immediately set aside whatever petty differences you have with your brother and stop playing silly games. To do otherwise in a situation such as this would be an outrage."

His mother's speech had little or no effect on Dalton. He yawned, stretched, and crossed the room to settle into a comfortable-looking armchair. "Whatever you say, Mother, but I am not my brother's keeper no matter how hard you crack that whip. As a lawyer though I would ask you one thing, as I'm sure our guests have already done, where is dear brother Connor? Don't tell me he's among the missing too! We're not to expect him to turn up in some nearby rose garden are we? Now that would be a coincidence."

Pritchard was apoplectic. "Dalton!"

Dalton folded his hands in front of him. "Does no one want to answer that one very important question? Where's Connor?"

Pritchard looked as though he was about to explode. "Your brother has gone off by himself for a while to clear his head."

Dalton actually laughed. "Oh, so he left town. Say, that is bad timing. Only guilty people run."

* * *

Connor noticed he was getting low on fuel. That was something he'd have to attend to in the morning.

He glanced at Maggie out of the corner of his eye and saw she was staring straight ahead out the windshield. If he didn't know any better, he'd guess she'd never been in an automobile before. She looked scared to death as they nipped along at the Model T's top speed of about forty miles per hour. He'd have to be careful when he got to Lancaster or for that matter Saint John, keep a lighter grip on the hand throttle. It was true he was a fast driver, but he liked the exhilaration of going quickly. It was freeing somehow, and he couldn't wait to take delivery of his new Model A Ford in Andalusite Blue. He'd been assured he could attain a top speed of about sixty-five miles per hour. Now *that* was a car. It briefly occurred to him the good times he would have in it.

And maybe he'd move to another city and start over, new car and all. He thought about his apprenticeship at McLagen & Son Ltd. He knew there were more interesting careers available, but he'd be the worst kind of fool to walk away from the family business. Some day it would all be his. Then he'd have a free hand to make the changes he wanted, and he had several in mind. He'd even made the mistake of mentioning them to his father, with predictable results. Pritchard McLagen was not into change.

His thoughts returned to Sarah and how he'd thought his life was going to work out even as recently as two days ago. He pushed her from his mind again.

"Is it much further?" asked Maggie interrupting his thoughts. "I need to use the washroom real bad."

Now there was a reality check. Women didn't usually mention such things in polite company and certainly not to a stranger. Maybe she was another modern woman. It was getting so a man didn't know where he stood anymore. More men had to start putting their foot down, let women know there was a limit as to how much they were prepared to tolerate. There were lines that should not be crossed. Sarah hadn't known where those lines were and so had repeatedly crossed them. *No!* he told himself fiercely. He could not think about Sarah, or he would fall to pieces. That awful floating feeling was back, like a storm in a wind tunnel and he fought to keep himself calm, slow his breathing.

He forced his attention back to the woman sitting beside him. "We'll be where we're going in just a few minutes," he told her in a voice that sounded like somebody else's.

"You seem to be a million miles away."

He compelled a smile to his lips. "Sorry. I have a lot on my mind."

He was tired, he didn't realize how much until he'd done all this driving. He'd see if he could get a room for the night in a smaller hotel downtown. It was late and that's the only place he could think of that would serve his immediate needs. A good night's sleep might clear his mind. Maggie didn't offer any comment when they pulled into the parking area located behind the hotel, so he assumed his choice of accommodation was okay with her.

x x x

After Agnes went up to bed Pritchard reread the newspaper story about the murder. At least it had succeeded in bumping the mobster trial off the front page. He himself was sick of hearing about the trials and tribulations of Prohibition. Not even Canada's upcoming Diamond Jubilee set to celebrate the country's sixtieth anniversary received worthy coverage. The murder of a beautiful young woman trumped all else. Nowhere in the headline story about Sarah could he find the name McLagen, although he knew it was only a matter of time before it too would become banner headlines ... probably mere hours because once the press got their teeth into the McLagen connection they'd be like a dog with a bone. They would never let it go and his family would be forced to withstand the ensuing public disgrace. How he had ever allowed girls who were not in the McLagen social set to attend his sons' parties was beyond him.

Anything went with young people nowadays because not just one of his sons had become infatuated with that Estey girl, they both had. She'd thrown one of them back and kept the other. Why did Dalton and Connor not understand that girls of lower class families were for dalliances only, one didn't marry them. They chose someone from their own social standing. But Sarah had been a beauty, a real prize. He'd give her that and so apparently all bets were off. In his day you sowed your wild oats, and he'd certainly sowed plenty of his own, before marrying someone socially acceptable. He'd never been sorry he'd taken Agnes for his bride. It was not only the proper thing to do, but he had actually fallen in love with her.

He thought again about his two sons, very different, but still his pride and joy. Would he lose one of them because of that Estey girl?

* * *

"I'm hungry!" Maggie complained once she'd tended to her immediate needs.

Connor looked at her as if seeing her for the first time. Her face was gaunt. "When was the last time you ate?"

She thought for a moment. "Day before yesterday. Can you get me something to eat before we...."

He shook his head in disbelief. "Yes, I'll get you something to eat. Now tell me, how did you come to be on the road ... on your way to Boston?"

Her eyes darted around the room, coming to rest on the double bed with its floral chenille spread. "I said Boston because it sounded good. I don't know where I'm going. I've got no money."

"Are you going to tell me why you were on that road?"

Her eyes flashed. "It's none of your business. Never mind the food, I've got to go," and with that she made for the door.

Connor was startled into action, seizing her from behind. "I'm sorry. I thought since I was going to buy you dinner and give you a place to sleep you might not mind telling me about yourself."

She didn't struggle against him, and that was good because he was certain now he didn't want to be alone. Maybe he'd already understood that, or he wouldn't have picked her up in the first place. It was insane but the thought of her leaving seemed almost too much to bear with everything else he was dealing with. Maybe he'd had all the rejection he could handle.

She frowned. "You ask too many questions. I don't ask questions. I don't even know your name."

"Enoch. My name is Enoch ... uh ... Whittaker. There, now you know me. Come on back over and sit down. I don't know what I can get to eat at this hour. We passed a little store just up the block that advertised lunch so maybe they'd still have something."

She relaxed visibly as she sat down beside him on the edge of the bed, before moving to a chair at the corner table a few feet away. "Whatever you can get I suppose. I'm not fussy."

He hadn't had anything to eat since breakfast that morning and he was hungry too, his usual robust appetite reasserting itself and demanding to be satisfied.

"All right, I'll see what I can come up with, if anything."

Her eyes told him she would be very easy to please when it came to food, the poor woman.

"Okay, that'd be good. And I'd like some milk to drink, unless you have something more interesting with you."

He had to smile at her temerity. "I have nothing more interesting than milk or water to offer you, that is if I can even get milk. You wait here and I'll be right back."

"All right," she agreed, still sitting stiffly in the chair.

If she was gone when he got back, he'd have lots of food to eat, and the way his appetite was beginning to kick in he might be able to manage it. The trick was to get it to stay down. He'd have to keep his mind off Sarah.

The store was small and poorly lit, but despite the hour he was indeed able to buy sandwiches, and two stale doughnuts. He had to admit he was spoiled when it came to doughnuts. Their cook, Lavinia Henderson, was outstandingly good in the kitchen. Her doughnuts were mouthwatering, there was no other way to describe them. These ones might have been better when they were made a week ago, but whatever. The food would fill their stomachs, but there would be no satisfaction in getting it there. Maggie would be glad about the milk though, a whole quart between them.

Once back in the room he set the paper bags on the table and joined her there, watching as she dove at her share without table manners. Never had he seen food disappear so quickly. She must have been half starved to even get through it because the sandwiches were dry as dust, the bread old and the doughnuts heavy with grease. But he did manage to eat his share of the meal. There were no other options on the immediate horizon, otherwise he wouldn't have touched any of it.

"Do you feel better?" he asked after she'd wiped her face and hands and settled back in the chair.

"Much better!" she answered with a smile. "I feel downright neighbourly now."

He chuckled. "What does that mean? I thought you were already being neighbourly."

She tilted her head and looked at him coquettishly, suddenly playful. "I mean I feel like getting to know you better. Oh, and thank you by the way. That food wasn't too bad."

He supposed that anything would be considered edible if you were hungry enough. "You're welcome."

She slipped out of her jacket and hung it on the back of the chair, then kicked off her shoes.

Connor knit his hands behind his head leaning back in his chair as he regarded her with a smile. "So you're not going to tell me about yourself?"

She held up a warning finger, her good mood suddenly headed south. "I told you, no questions!"

He was not to be shut down that easily. "I think I get to ask you at least one question. After all, I did buy you dinner and it seems you and I are about to get to know one another ... better. Come on, Maggie, why all the secrets?"

She regarded him speculatively. "Why do you need to know about me? What about you? For all *I* know you could be a bank robber or a murderer. Why don't we start there? Tell me something about *yourself*. Where do you get all your money? You've got a nice car and you dress real fine. Maybe you're the one with something to hide."

He laughed although he was aware it sounded hollow. "Okay, fair enough. Maybe we don't need to know everything about each other if all we're going to do is spend a few hours together."

She nodded. "My thinking exactly," she said as she began to unbutton her blouse.

Well hello, Maggie! He'd thought maybe they'd talk for a while and then let whatever was going to happen, happen. But she was obviously much more experienced in these sorts of things than he was. But crazily enough he wanted her to do it for the right reasons, not because she thought she owed him something for a couple of bad sandwiches.

"Maggie, stop," he said, holding up his hand. "You don't have to do this if you don't want to. I think you feel like you do because I bought you some food. You don't. You can stay here for the night if you want to. I'm guessing you don't have anywhere else to go, but you don't have to sleep with me."

She had already slipped out of her blouse, and he was struck by how thin she was under her clothes, completely unattractive. Poor Maggie looked as though she had seen the hard side of life and he didn't want to be one more man taking advantage of her.

"Are you serious? I know I owe you and debts have to be paid. You brought me here for one reason and that's what we're about to take care of. Are you telling me you don't want to be with me?"

Maggie had probably paid a lot of debts, none of which had gotten her anywhere in life except on her back.

He was about to answer when there was a loud knock on the door. Now who in creation could that be at this hour? Who knew he was here? It occurred to him, ridiculously, that it might be his father. That notion was quickly discarded when he opened the door and saw two men standing there.

The older, stocky officer spoke first, and he didn't look like a man to be fooled with. Neither did the other one for that matter. "Connor McLagen?"

Connor looked from one to the other. "Yes, that's me," he said as he felt his strength drain out of him.

Both men stepped into the room, Connor reflexively backing up out of their way.

The taller man eyed Maggie disdainfully, her blouse held up in front of her, before returning his attention to the object of their visit.

"Connor McLagen," he repeated, "you're under arrest for the murder of Sarah Estey. Turn around and put your hands behind your back."

Chapter Eleven

Connor's instinctive reaction was to run, a knee-pumping all out dash to somewhere ... anywhere but here. He realized as sanity returned how futile that attempt at flight would be. He was in the middle of a nightmare with no apparent way out.

He felt the blood drain from his face. "Murder?" he asked stupidly. "I didn't murder anyone, let alone Sarah."

The taller detective snapped the handcuffs shut once Connor had provided his hands for the procedure.

A few feet away Maggie pivoted, jamming her arms into her blouse, and buttoning it before turning back to face the men.

The second detective regarded her with contempt. "Who are you?"

She pointed to Connor. "I had supper with him."

The tall detective smirked. "Do you always undress to eat?"

Surprisingly, she flushed as she grabbed her jacket and pulled that on too. "Of course not."

The second officer continued to stare at her. "How long have you known this man?" he asked with a head gesture toward Connor.

She looked as pale as Connor felt. "About an hour or so, maybe two. He said his name was Enoch ... ummm ... Whittaker. That's it, Enoch Whittaker, and I'm Maggie Strong from Saint John."

The shorter detective huffed a chuckle, rolling forward on the balls of his feet. "Well Maggie, you know now he's not Enoch anybody. I think you'd better come downtown with us too."

She looped her shoulder bag into place, still staring saucer-eyed at Connor. "He's wanted for murder?" she asked. "I didn't know anything about that. I never saw him before today, honestly."

Mortified, Connor watched her. "She's telling the truth and so am I. She hasn't done anything wrong, and I didn't murder anyone."

The first detective studied Maggie. "How did you two get together?"

Her face darkened as she folded her arms defensively across her chest, now seemingly ready to do battle. Poor Maggie had probably been fighting most of her life. "I was walking on the road when he came along and offered me a drive...."

The first detective rolled his eyes. "And you offered him something else, is that about how it went? Or was it love at first sight?"

She pinned him with a glare. "There's no law that says a man and a woman can't get together if they want to, is there? He was very nice to me."

The tall detective wasn't giving any ground. "There's a law against streetwalking, but I'm pretty sure you already know about that."

She glowered at him. "I am not a streetwalker! There was never any mention of money."

The detective didn't react. "Yeah sure, but you're coming with us until we check you out. Come on."

The first detective had a vicelike grip on Connor's upper arm propelling him forward. "Let's go, lover boy."

Connor could feel panic surging through him like a live thing. "I'm telling you, you're mistaken. I didn't murder anyone! And what about my car? We can't leave it here. It could get stolen."

The tall detective looked as though he was about to use up the last of his patience. "Leave it where it is, it's fine."

Soon all four were underway for the relatively short walk to the central police station on King Street East.

Once Maggie had been checked out, she was let go with a warning and practically ran out of the police station, apparently unafraid of the dark as she hurried down Carmarthen Street. Connor was not so fortunate, now sitting in a claustrophobic windowless room just big enough for himself and the two detectives. It was a tight fit as the questioning began.

"I'm Detective Frank London," the taller of the two men introduced himself, "and this is Detective Peter Halverson. You are to answer our questions truthfully. Believe me, we'll know when you're lying, and we don't like it when people lie to us."

Halverson, himself no slouch in the size department, leaned across the table until he was inches from Connor's face. "Why did you kill her, Connor? Did the little lady say no to you? Did she want to wait for her wedding night, and you didn't and things got a little rough maybe? She wasn't very big, probably didn't take much to shut her up, did it?"

Connor felt sick, swallowing hard to keep his nausea in check. "Nothing like that happened. The last time I saw my fiancé she was very much alive."

"She was still *alive*. Does that mean the fight had already happened and she just hadn't died yet? Is that what you're telling us?"

Connor felt like crying. "I only found out she was dead this afternoon when I saw it in the newspaper. I didn't even know she'd called off the wedding until Wednesday night. I was in a state of shock when her mother showed me the note. I'm still in a state of shock."

London studied him. "In such a state of shock that you were ready to jump into bed with the first old bag you found? Why didn't you stay home? Why did you go running off like you did if you didn't have anything to do with your fiancé's death? You're lying."

Connor was completely at sea. "I'm not lying. I tell you I was in shock. I didn't know what to do with myself. I know it looks bad, but I didn't do anything wrong. Maybe I was trying to outrun memories, I don't know. I can hardly think straight at the moment."

Halverson leaned in closer too. "Bad memories you mean? Like doing murder?"

Connor struggled to keep his wits about him and not let himself get trapped, but these two men were unnerving him. They were practiced at intimidation although he understood intellectually why they acted as they did. They were used to dealing with some pretty rough characters. For all they knew he was a killer. How did he expect them to act? Like old friends at a country club? Didn't all innocent people think they should be dealt with decently? But these men had probably heard every argument in the book, a million lies because they were in the line of work where people routinely lied to them. How were they to know he was an honourable man? It was up to him to convince them.

"I didn't murder Sarah!" Connor said as forcefully as he dared. "The last time I saw her was Monday night. I went to her home on Wednesday night, last night I guess it was, and took a bouquet of flowers because Sarah and I...."

London folded his arms. "Sarah and you, what?"

Connor took a deep breath. "I loved my fiancé, or my ex-fiancé I guess she ended up being."

London's stare was penetrating. "Sarah and you, what? Was there something wrong between you? You have a fight?"

Connor looked away first, unable to hold his stare, aware that when he did so it would make him appear evasive. "I thought everything was fine with her."

Halverson took the lead. "You're lying. Everything was not fine, was it? Tell us what happened. Tell us everything. You're not going anywhere until you do, so you might as well make up your mind to it."

Connor was determined to make them see reason. "Every couple has problems, but they work through them. I loved Sarah and I was trying to forgive...."

He knew the moment the words were out of his mouth he had incriminated himself. Provided the necessary ammunition to charge him with murder. He could tell by the look of these two bloodhounds they were determined to pin this on him, and he was making it easy.

Connor raised his voice out of frustration. "Look, I did not have anything to do with the death of my fiancé. I don't even know when she was killed. You have to believe me!"

Halverson watched Connor closely. "No, we don't have to believe you at all because we know you're not being honest with us. This isn't a Rothesay tea party. You're looking at a murder charge. Now, what did you have to forgive your fiancé for?"

Connor was silent. How had he ever made that slip?

Halverson moved closer. "Forgive her for what, Connor? What did she do to you that made you mad enough to kill her?"

Connor took another deep steadying breath, trying to choose his words carefully. "I was trying to forgive her for being with someone else if you want the truth, but that had happened before I ever met her. I didn't like the idea of what she did is all, but it's hardly something you kill someone for. That's a ridiculous assumption!"

Halverson never took his eyes off Connor. "It depends on how much you didn't like it. I think you didn't like it a lot. I think you were going to make her pay for it. Weren't you?"

Moving closer, London unexpectedly reached in back of Connor and undid the cuffs. "Put your hands on the table in front of you. Lay them flat!"

Connor complied, his arms stiff and aching from the tight shackles.

London reached down and took hold of Connor's right hand, straightening it out none too gently. "Is that how you hurt your hand, lover boy? It looks sore to me."

Connor winced. "I slammed it in the car door. I was upset when I left Sarah's house Wednesday night and misjudged the door's width. That's all it was, a stupid mistake."

London looked at Halverson and made a mock pity face. "I hate it when they slam their hand in the car door, don't you Pete? That's gotta hurt. The problem is, I don't think he slammed it in the car door at all. I think it happened when he was fighting with Sarah, don't you?"

Halverson nodded. "Yeah, that's what I think happened too. Listen, lover boy, you're starting to get on our nerves, so why don't you tell us what happened and get it over with? You know you want to get it out of your system. I hear confession is good for the soul, so you're going to feel a whole lot better when you get it off your chest. I'm going to get you a nice big piece of paper and a nice sharp pencil and you can write it out for us, draw pictures if you want to. Tell us all the nasty details so we can get this thing wrapped up. You've got a hangman waiting for you, my friend. That's how this thing is going to end, you dangling on the end of a rope. That's what they do to men who kill women."

Connor tried to calm himself. "I will not confess to something I did not do. I would never have harmed Sarah. I loved her. Yes, we were having problems, but we might have been able to work them out. I don't know, but I'm an innocent man I tell you!"

London held himself in an attitude of disbelief. "Why did you run then if you're so innocent? You gotta admit it looks very bad for you."

Connor was becoming frantic. "I've already told you I wasn't running. I wanted to clear my head, that's all. I was still reeling about the broken engagement and Sarah leaving town. It made me crazy. I didn't know what to do with myself. Maybe I was worried people would think I'd done it after I read about it in the newspaper. That you'd come to my house."

London coughed and even that was aggressive. "No, we came to your hotel room instead, and what do we find from the man who says he loved his fiancé? We find a woman getting undressed to go to bed with him. That's how much you're missing Sarah. You were already moving on after your fiancé was out of the way. You did it all right. You're as guilty as sin. You don't fool us."

London left the room, snapping the door shut behind him. A moment later he was back, slamming several sheets of white paper and a pencil on the table in front of him. "Okay now, lover boy, start writing and don't leave anything out. You can start with *I killed Sarah Estey....*"

Connor could not hold back the tears as they came, hot and painful. "I. did. not. kill. Sarah! I had no reason to! I loved her!"

Halverson nodded his head slowly. "Oh, you did it all right. Innocent people don't run away, people with nothing to hide that is."

"If I was running away like you say, I didn't go very far, did I? I was right in Saint John for all the world to see. If I had cause to run away, I would have continued on to St. Stephen which is where I met Maggie ... on the road to St. Stephen. I would have crossed the border and kept on going, but no, I turned around and came back. Why would I do that if I was scared of getting caught?"

"Why? Could it be because you're stupid? You were running all right, you were just trying to figure out which direction you wanted to go, and you brought lots of cash to throw around, especially for women. And you didn't even pick a decent one. Took the first one you found on the side of the road if what she said is true."

He knew they were right about all of it because he had been going to sleep with that woman. Her only redeeming feature it seemed was that she'd been willing. He couldn't even explain it to himself. It was as though he went someplace else in his mind, became someone he didn't recognize ... or even want to. Perhaps it was his coping mechanism, but he had to admit all of it was damning. Maybe he and Sarah wouldn't have gotten married, but they could have hashed the whole thing out once and for all and possibly parted on friendly terms.

Maybe in his mind sleeping with Maggie would even the score between he and Sarah. After all, hadn't she slept with someone and broken his heart? If he did the same thing, he could no longer hold it over her that she hadn't waited for him. That's all the sense he could make of why he'd behaved the way he did. But he wasn't as terrible as they were making him out to be. He had given Maggie a way out if she wanted it. He had in no way forced her to stay with him. He was aware the entire situation looked idiotic, but then again nothing was making much sense at the moment.

London pursed his lips. "Tell me, lover boy, were there other women that maybe your fiancé found out about and she wasn't too happy? You had a little something else on the side and the whole thing blew up in your face?"

This time he reddened, and he felt that too, the rush of heat. He knew they saw it and it'd be interpreted as guilt. His already dismal mood sank even lower. "No, there was no one else. I did not cheat on Sarah."

Halverson's eyes were as cold as ice. "You're lying to us! I can smell it off you! Who was she? I want a name."

"She's an old friend," Connor admitted miserably before realizing he was incriminating Gladys. Maybe he should shut up and stop trying to cooperate. "I'm only telling you if it will help clear me, but I want her left out of this."

Halverson shook his head. "Boy you're a first-class schmuck, aren't you? You went after Sarah for what she'd done and you're ten times worse. Did this other woman help you kill your fiancé?"

"No!" Connor shouted. "I tell you she had nothing to do with it!"

London seized on Connor's mistake. "So you did it all on your own did you?"

Connor felt white-hot fury race through him. "My friend did not help me because I didn't do anything to need help with. I'm devastated someone killed Sarah, but it wasn't me."

Halverson snorted his derision. "You're devastated all right, but only because you got caught. What's her name, this *other* friend of yours?"

Connor shook his head. "I'm not going to tell you because she's an innocent bystander, someone I used to go out with before I met Sarah."

"An innocent bystander," Halverson parroted. "Have you seen this innocent bystander … oh … say in the last week or so?"

Connor was loathe to answer, but he had to make them understand. "I saw her Monday night, but we just talked. She called me. She was hoping we could get back together again but I told her I was getting married. She accepted my answer and that was the end of it."

London sighed. "But *you* were involved, weren't you, Connor?"

Connor was reaching the end of his rope as the hours continued to tick by, doing his best to stay alert. "Look, I am innocent. I did not commit any crime. Can't you see how torn up I am about Sarah's death? I'm in mourning! It's horrible that she's dead, but it was as much a surprise to me as it is to you."

London looked at Halverson and both shrugged. "I don't think he was surprised, Pete. Do you think he was surprised?"

Halverson made a face that said how seriously he took Connor. "I don't think he's surprised at all because he's sitting right here in front of us stinking up the room with his guilty conscience. You talk a good story but we're not buying one word of it because you were the last person seen with her before she died. Now write that confession out and stop wasting our time."

Connor folded his arms. "I'm not writing anything. I refuse to confess to something I didn't do no matter how much you browbeat me."

London moved like lightning, pounding his fist on the table. "Write that confession, now! You murdered her and you know you did! Be a man for once in your life and stop riding on Daddy's coattails. Swallow your pill instead of trying to blame it on the boogeyman. No one else had a reason to harm that girl, no motive, except you. She'd done something you didn't like, and you couldn't handle it. You were also running around on her, and she didn't like that so you let her have it for both those reasons. You can't change that, but you can make it right by owning up to it. Take responsibility for your actions. Start writing, McLagen. We'll leave you alone for a few minutes, but when we come back there'd better be something on that paper or we're going to start playing hardball. We've been nice up 'til now and I guarantee you don't want to be around us when we're not nice. We don't like liars, we don't like scapegoats, and we don't like murderers ... especially of women."

Connor felt as though he was going to be sick to his stomach, that greasy mess he'd eaten earlier roiling around in his gut at full speed. Why oh why had he taken off the way he did this afternoon? Naturally he looked guilty to the police. Anyone with half a brain would make the same assumption. Not much wonder they thought he was lying. He'd never felt such fear in his life, his clothes drenched with sweat in the airless room.

More time passed agonizingly slowly. Connor guessed it to be at least mid-morning by now. He was emotionally drained, physically and mentally exhausted, and enduring the agony of trying to stay awake. It was torturous. Still they kept up the pressure.

Except for a couple of bathroom breaks he'd been in this hard wooden chair the whole time, his captors' unrelenting. He knew if it was him looking in, he'd probably assume he was guilty too because of how he'd handled everything. Leaving the way he did was one of the stupidest ideas he'd ever had in his life. Also, because he'd told his father he was going away for a few days, he very likely didn't even know his son was in police custody. If he did, he would likely intervene although he doubted the McLagens would have enough influence to get him out of this. Provincial liquor inspectors were one thing, murder was something else altogether.

London marched back into the room, his partner on his heels, the door slamming behind them. He shoved the paper toward Connor again. "Start writing, lover boy! This doesn't stop until you confess. You think you're tough? I promise you, sonny, we're a lot tougher. We'll break you before you ever break us."

"Stop calling me lover boy!" Connor seethed, a headache pounding in his temples.

London pulled a sympathetic face. "Oh, he doesn't like the name we gave him," he said to his partner before returning his attention to Connor. "That's your name. It fits. You like to love them then kill them. Was ole Maggie next? Maybe we got there just in time."

Connor was trembling from exhaustion. "I've never harmed another human being in my life. It's not in me to kill ... anybody!" he shouted.

Coming around the table, Halverson sneered in his face. "It's in everybody to kill, it's just a question of why, and the opportunity to do it. That's all. You killed her all right, it's written all over you, lover boy. At least have the guts to admit it."

Connor shook his head. "You keep saying I killed Sarah, that I know I did. I don't even know how she died. I don't even own a gun, so how could I kill her?"

The two interrogators exchanged a brief glance. "You know how you killed her. Do you think this is the first time we've been on this merry-go-round? No! We're used to people lying to try to save themselves, but in the end the truth comes out whether they trip themselves up or get tired of lying. Then we get the confession. You're new at this. We're not. You're not as smart as you think you are, not even by half. Now come on, you know how she died because you were there with her when it happened. Stop lying!"

Connor was near his breaking point. "I don't know how she died because I didn't kill her. Why would I kill her? I loved her I tell you. I'll say it as many times as I have to because it's the truth. Whether we ended up getting married or not, that would not have changed."

London regarded Connor malevolently. "You know, lover boy, you should make your confession now while you're still dealing with us. The men coming in next will make us look like choirboys. You think it's been tough so far? This will look like a Sunday school picnic compared to what's ahead if you don't spill the beans. Your choice."

* * *

The fact that Connor was being questioned had indeed been made known. That afternoon's headlines were emblazoned across the front page of the newspaper announcing Connor was in police custody. The newsboy was yelling himself hoarse as to the latest sensational development in this high-profile murder case. His soiled white newspaper bag was emptying fast, the crowd quickly snapping up the afternoon edition.

* * *

Cranston Estey straightened his evening newspaper, furiously shaking out the folds before adjusting his rimless spectacles and starting to read.

"I knew Connor McLagen killed Sarah, I just knew it," he announced with satisfaction. "I could tell by the look of him he was no good. It was just a question of time before he got down to business. I'm surprised she lived as long as she did keeping his company."

Maude set the plate of beef cold cuts on the table, not looking at her husband. "I don't believe Connor did it," she bravely disagreed. "Why would he come here with flowers for her if she was already dead? He was shocked when I showed him the note and I believe it was a genuine reaction."

Cranston lowered the paper, glaring at her. "Sometimes you are unbelievably stupid, Maude. Did you expect him to come right out and confess it to you of all people? Liars play the game of deception, and he played it about as well as most."

She wanted to ask him how he came to be so knowledgeable about such things but ignored his jibe. "It's the most frightful thing to think about someone taking her life," she continued, her voice wavering. "My only hope, my only prayer is that she didn't suffer. That it was over quickly, however it happened."

He shook his head. "Again, astonishingly naïve. Killers want their victims to suffer, that's what they enjoy the most."

She looked at him with new eyes. Why had she never noticed that side of him before, his alarming emotional detachment? It was very strange. She wondered if she should be frightened of him. He'd been rough with her, but nothing of any real consequence as in threatening to kill her. But then again everyone was on edge she imagined, considering the events of the past few days.

And she meant what she'd said about Connor. There was a gut feeling that wouldn't go away that he had not harmed Sarah. His reaction to seeing the note had been genuine, she'd bet her life it had not been feigned. No one was that good an actor. Yet he was the one they had in custody and if no other suspects were found he could be convicted of her murder and executed.

Cranston lifted the paper again and continued reading, stopping moments later. "And this inane rag of a newspaper is so caught up in the whole business they'll print anything. Most of what they're saying is speculation. Look at what they've said about me! That I chose not to serve my country in the First World War and that's a bunch of poppycock! They make me look unpatriotic! I could not serve for medical reasons, otherwise I certainly would have. I have a sterling reputation. Let me just say if I could get hold of Connor McLagen right now, I'd kill him with my bare hands for the disgrace he's brought upon me."

"Maybe you should have talked to those newspaper reporters when they called," Maude ventured. "That could be why it's wrong."

"I would never speak to people like that!" Cranston declared with typical vehemence. "My life is none of their business. I hold *all* newspapers in contempt."

'Then what do you expect?' she wanted to say, but wisely held her tongue.

* * *

Thomas Chaffee leaned heavily against the upper deck railing, the salty breeze cool on his face and playing catch me if you can with his hair. He'd so looked forward to his furlough, a much-needed rest from his service in the mission field. Mostly he'd looked forward to seeing Sarah again. He'd always felt that someday his attraction to her would culminate in marriage, his undying love finally come to fruition. It didn't matter she'd said she didn't love him. Sometimes love had to have a chance to grow, and he was convinced hers would have.

Reverend Estey had practically assured him he could persuade his daughter to marry him and move to Africa. So he'd hurried back to New Brunswick, but that had not been the case. To be denied after all these long years of waiting was too much to bear.

He'd been in love with Sarah since she was a girl. He'd never acted on those sometimes overwhelming urges, instead biding his time until she came of age and then the plum would be ripe for the picking. But things hadn't gone according to plan, and he'd failed miserably. The disappointment had been so great he'd temporarily lost his head and done something he'd regret for the rest of his life, God forgive him. At the moment he didn't see how he could possibly go on.

"Sir, are you all right?"

He turned sharply to see a deck officer watching him with concern. "Errr ... yes. I'm fine. Just a bit distracted, I guess. Why do you ask?"

The officer took hold of Thomas' arm and directed him to a deck chair, then sat down beside him. "You've been standing at that rail for more than an hour staring at the water. Are you sure you're all right?"

Thomas managed to get control of his emotions. "I'm fine thank you. I have something on my mind. I don't have any intentions of jumping," he added when the officer didn't appear to be convinced. "I believe I'll go below now and have a little rest."

The officer watched Thomas as he cleared the upper deck in long strides and disappeared through the hatchway.

* * *

Connor was alone again, presumably to think, to come to his senses about confessing. Instead, he laid his head on his hands feeling on the point of collapse, his mind fogged by drowsiness.

He thought about Dalton. He knew his brother was still in love with Sarah, and he should have taken him to task about it more forcefully than he did. But that was water under the bridge now, a missed opportunity. He wondered if Dalton was capable of harming her? Murdering her? Dalton was spoiled, that much was apparent. He also knew what his brother was like if he didn't get his way, but kill someone? He couldn't see it. He was tempted to tell them about Dalton giving Sarah a ride home on Monday night. He remembered his own conversation with her a short time later. She'd made everything sound innocent enough, but something had taken place in Dalton's car. He'd bet his life on it. But what could he do about it? He couldn't sell out his own brother.

* * *

Neither Pritchard nor Agnes McLagen was home when the police arrived to execute a search warrant at Orchard Hill, and Evelyn the new maid saw no reason not to allow the nice officers in for a look around. What better way to clear the handsome young Connor than to let the police see he had nothing to hide? She couldn't imagine that her employers would mind her doing so, it was important they cooperate with the police wasn't it, so the real killer could be found? This whole murder business was enormously upsetting for everyone involved.

The search took less than two hours, and she was surprised when they approached her carrying a pair of muddy shoes. What on earth would they want with those?

"Do these belong to Connor McLagen?" the first officer asked.

Evelyn shook her head embarrassed it seemed by their find. "I meant to clean those, but it's been a busy day. No, officer, those shoes don't belong to Connor, they belong to Dalton McLagen and I have no idea how they got to be in such a mess."

Chapter Twelve

Connor sat with his head in his hands, thoroughly disheartened. Still alone, he thought about Sarah as her death began to hit home, never mind the enormity of his current predicament. He'd tried to push the horror of her murder out of his mind, but he couldn't pretend any longer she wasn't gone.

Funny, what he'd previously thought were insurmountable problems between them now seemed inconsequential. He'd made too much of her fling with another man. Yes, it still hurt, but it was in the past and he should have left it there. He'd give anything to have that situation back again. Boy, would he handle it differently!

He felt the tears come again, coursing down his cheeks. He thought of Sarah's life being taken away with brute force. How she must have suffered. He fought to keep the bile from rising in his throat. If he ever got his hands on whoever had done this terrible thing, he *would* do murder and have no problem taking responsibility for it. Sarah was tiny, but he knew she'd put up a fight if she'd had the chance. He thrust vile images of how she might have died out of his mind.

And *when* had she died? He wasn't even sure about that. And now here he sat, accused of her murder. He was heartsick at her loss, but unwilling to sacrifice his own life to pay for a crime he hadn't committed.

He didn't lift his head when he heard the door open and then close with a perfunctory snap, the scrape of the chair being pulled out on the other side of the table. London remained standing but Halverson sat down opposite Connor and in his face. He braced himself for another onslaught.

"Connor, are you ready to tell us what happened?" he asked in a calm voice. "I don't think you even meant to kill her, did you?"

It seemed Halverson had abandoned his tough guy approach, now using the *just between us guys* tact, urging him to unburden himself. Have it over with. Go to meet his Maker with a clear conscience.

Connor raised his head, wiping at his eyes with the sleeves of his shirt. "I don't even know when she was killed. Can you tell me that much?"

Halverson waited a moment before he spoke. "You tell *me*, Connor. I wasn't there. You were."

"I probably would tell you if I knew. The last time I talked to Sarah was when we had that set to on Monday night. As I've already said, I went over to her house with flowers to apologize a couple of days later, and that's when her mother showed me the note saying the wedding was off. I can guess it was during that intervening time, I still don't know exactly when it happened. Have they finished the autopsy? That should indicate the approximate time of death, shouldn't it? If I knew when it was, I probably have an alibi."

London studied the suspect. "Come on, Connor, the game is up. Now *you* tell *me* when she died, or have you conveniently forgotten when that was?"

Connor shook his head. "How could I forget when I don't know?"

London seemed to be taking his measure. "All right, as near as they can determine it was sometime Tuesday and since she was at school all that day, it was likely Tuesday night. Now, does that jog your memory?"

Connor stared at him. "I can account for all of Tuesday, and Tuesday night and Wednesday for that matter."

Halverson sighed. "Connor, don't bother cooking up any more stories. We have a witness who says she saw you pick Sarah up on Tuesday evening about seven o'clock to drive her home. She said she heard you and Sarah arguing."

Connor stared at him. Who would say such a thing? "Whoever told you that is not telling the truth. It never happened. I was at work on Tuesday evening."

London sat back and folded his arms across his chest. "One of you is lying. Let's hear this alibi of yours, we're all ears."

Connor explained how he was at McLagen & Son all day Tuesday and worked late on Tuesday evening, which, he explained, could be verified by his father's secretary because she'd been there too along with his father. Also, he'd been travelling with his father that day and after work they'd driven straight home. He hadn't left home until Wednesday morning and again he'd travelled with his father into the city to work. He had an alibi for the time when Sarah had been murdered.

Halverson listened intently, taking notes before returning Connor's hopeful gaze. "We're going to check this out, and if it turns out you're lying to us, which I think you are, it will go badly for you. I would suggest if you are lying, tell me now and I'll tear up this piece of paper. I'll also tell you if we're unable to check out your story, we will be formally charging you with the murder of Sarah Estey."

Not a religious man, Connor felt the need to pray as both detectives left the room and he was alone with his thoughts once again. He thought about Dalton. Why had he not come to try to get him released? And where was his father's influence? Surely he must know by now he'd been arrested and was going through hell. He'd never felt so alone in his life.

* * *

Halverson placed a phone call to the Frederick Hobson residence and luckily found Fanny at home.

"Fanny, when we talked to you, you told us you had seen Connor McLagen pick Sarah up at your place on Tuesday evening, after you and Sarah returned from Saint John. He was going to drive her home you said, but he tells us he was never there. Are you certain it was Connor McLagen? Remember before you answer there is a man's life on the line. If you made a mistake about what you told us, now is the time to correct it."

She hesitated long enough that he knew she was going to change her story, and he was right.

"Honestly, it was down by the end of the driveway, so it was a fair distance from where I was standing. It looked like Connor's car, a black Model T, so I naturally assumed it was him. Now that I think about it again it could have been the same kind of car owned by somebody else. She must have known who it was though because she got in the car and left with them. There are quite a few cars like his around so I guess I couldn't actually swear under oath it was Connor. I'm sorry."

"You said you heard his voice, heard them arguing."

There was another telling pause. "Well, I heard voices. Perhaps I was a bit hasty in assuming it was Connor, but I did hear someone speaking loudly. Am I in trouble for getting this wrong, officer? I'm really very sorry."

Halverson sighed tiredly. God save him from recanting witnesses. "It's important we get it right. Thank you, Miss Hobson."

He then dialled McLagen & Son Ltd.

* * *

It seemed like hours before he heard footsteps approaching and Halverson and London re-entered the room. His hopes began to rise cautiously, fuelled by their expressions. Could it be disappointment he saw on their faces? Maybe it was because they obviously wanted to solve this murder. Tying everything up quickly would look good for them.

"You're free to go," London told him, holding the door open. "Your alibi checked out."

Halverson looked like a junkyard dog deprived of his bite. "Yeah, your alibi checked out. You might think you're out of the woods, but you're not. You might not have done the deed yourself, but we believe you know who did. We're not buying your act, tears and all. Go on, get out of here but don't leave town. We'll be watching you and if you do leave, you'll be back here before you can say jack."

Connor got to his feet on a fresh shot of adrenalin as though they might change their minds and put him back in cuffs. It was indeed like waking up after a night terror and he wasted no time heading for the door.

* * *

Dalton was in the middle of dictating a letter to his secretary when a knock sounded on his office door. Annoyed at the interruption he got up to answer it, surprised to see the police.

"If you're looking for my brother, Connor, he's not here, gentlemen," he told them.

Halverson was in his junkyard dog mood. "Are you Dalton McLagen?"

Dalton stiffened. "I am."

Halverson's focus was razor sharp with no patience it seemed for dandies as he introduced himself and his partner. "Then you're the one we're looking for, come with us. We're taking you downtown for questioning in the murder of Sarah Estcy."

Dalton's attempt at humour did not meet with favour. "I'm already downtown. Now if you'll excuse me...."

It was London's turn. "You can come along with us quietly ... or not. We can accommodate you another way, be happy to in fact."

Dalton glanced back at the secretary who'd been watching the proceedings before quickly turning her head to pretend otherwise. "That will be all, Nellie," Dalton told her tightly. "We'll finish that letter when I get back."

The young woman left the office without a backward glance.

Dalton returned his attention to the officers. "Give me a moment and I'll come with you and we can get this whole thing straightened out."

He made his way to his most senior partner's office and explained he had a personal matter requiring his immediate attention. He did not reveal the nature of his absence, and thankfully Nellie was not prone to gossip. He knew she'd be pleasantly surprised when he returned within the hour and got back down to business. Murder investigation indeed!

Dalton walked out with his head held high until he was out of earshot of the office, then turned on his escorts. "I suppose my brother has been filling your heads with all sorts of foolishness."

Halverson kept pace with the others, despite his shorter stride. "Actually he never mentioned you."

Dalton smiled at an acquaintance they passed on the street, as though he was out for an afternoon stroll with two of Saint John's finest. "I'd like to believe that's true."

Within minutes they were at the police station and in the very room vacated earlier by his younger brother.

Dalton walked in and took a seat with an affected demeanour that clearly said: *I'm above all this.*

London closed the door. "We've brought you here, Mr. McLagen, because we have reason to believe you were involved in the Sarah Estey murder."

Dalton nodded. "So you mentioned. And what on earth makes you think that?"

Halverson left the room and returned with Dalton's muddy shoes. "Seems you've been doing a little gardening. One wouldn't think you'd wear your best shoes to bury someone but then again, those things can get unexpectedly messy."

Dalton laughed, but it was more like the sound of profound relief. "Is that it? That's your evidence against me? Talk about low hanging fruit."

Halverson fixed Dalton with an icy stare. "Explain them being in that condition, or do you work as a gardener on the side?"

Dalton held up his hands. "Listen. A friend of mine is building a new home overlooking the river and is now in the process of landscaping it. He invited me out to see the work and I must say he's done a fine job, but the grounds were a caution. It was quite muddy because of that downpour the other night. He apologized for the mess of my shoes, but I told him it was no bother. I guess our maid, Evelyn hasn't gotten around to cleaning them yet." Dalton got to his feet. "Now, if you'll excuse me."

Halverson pointed to the chair. "Not so fast. What's the name of the *friend* who's doing all this landscaping?"

Dalton shrugged. "I can give you his name *and* address. I should mention he's also a colleague of mine. His office is next door to mine at the law firm. You could have saved a lot of extra bother if you'd brought the shoes along to my office." He pointed to the muddy footwear sitting on the table. "If you have a bag, I'll take those with me. I'll ask Evelyn to spruce them up tonight."

London's face had turned to stone. "Sit down! We're not done here by a long shot. What is your colleague's telephone number? We'll call him and have a nice talk, so you might as well get comfortable. You're going to be here for awhile."

Dalton crossed his arms, thoroughly annoyed now. "I don't see why...."

London's stare would freeze water. "Sit down!"

Dalton reclaimed his chair, tamping down anger. Snatching up the sheet of paper left over from Connor's interrogation, he wrote down his colleague's telephone number. He shoved it toward Halverson who picked it up, read it then left the room presumably to make the call.

Dalton's mood continued to deteriorate. "This is ridiculous! I won't be treated like this, and I refuse to answer any more questions."

London's smile never reached his eyes. "Yeah, that's what all the guilty ones say because they have something to hide."

"I have nothing to hide, and I refuse to be drawn into this little Keystone Cops adventure. You're running around arresting whomever you choose and you won't get away with this. My father is a very influential man."

London was not intimidated. "Yeah, I know who your father is, and his money doesn't mean anything to me."

Dalton felt panic begin to lap at him. "I had nothing to do with that Estey bitch. She was my brother's fiancé, my brother's problem. You know as well as I do, he did it. Who else would have reason to?"

London didn't seem to be listening, instead studying the man seated before him. "How did you get that cut on your lip, Mr. McLagen?"

Dalton waved him off. "Oh that, I cut myself shaving. It stung like hell."

London leaned in for a closer look. "Nah, that's no shaving cut, not on your lip like that and it's bruised." He looked even closer. "And it looks like you've tried to cover the bruise with make-up. Wet your thumb and run it over the cut."

"I will not! What happens to my face is no concern of yours."

"Oh, but it is." London, a born pacer, walked a few steps away before turning. "She fought you, did she?"

Dalton reddened to the roots of his hair. Yes, Sarah had fought back, and his lip still throbbed where she'd connected with that diamond ring. It must have pleased her to mark him like that. He was lucky though. It had looked a lot worse a couple of days ago.

"I asked you a question, McLagen."

"I don't run around murdering people. So no, I never killed her if that's what you want to know."

"Are you saying you fought with her, but you didn't expect her to die? But she did die and then you had to do something with the body. Am I starting to get warm?"

"That's a nice story, but it's a fairy tale. There was no fight, no dying and certainly no burying, not that had anything to do with me."

"Sarah Estey is very much dead, and to get that way someone had to kill her."

"I'm telling you it wasn't me. I'm not your man. And while you're wasting time here with me, the real killer is getting away. Did that ever occur to you?"

"No, I think the real killer is sitting right in this room with us. Now tell me what happened to you. How'd you get that busted lip? And don't tell me it happened at your friend's house. That you didn't like his landscaping job after all, and he popped you one."

Dalton folded his arms and looked away. "Let's just say if you do decide to charge me, which would be a huge mistake, I can tell you right now a pair of muddy shoes will not hold up in court. You'd look even stupider than you actually are if that's all the evidence you have. You could go out onto the street in front of this place right now and round up at least a dozen people with dirty shoes. Heaven only knows why you decided to pick on me. Your detective skills are a little rusty if that's as good as you've got."

"You've got a fresh mouth. Now suppose you tell me how you hurt it?"

"I told you I cut it shaving."

London laughed, but it was not in the interests of humour. "What do you use to shave, a meat cleaver?"

Dalton, eyes narrowed, unfolded his arms and leaned forward. "I've got a piece of advice for you. Don't give up your police job and try to be a Vaudeville comedian. You're not very funny, even when you try."

London took an ominous step closer. "And if you don't want a matching bruise on the other side of your mouth, I'd watch myself if I were you, or would I be too much for you? Are women more your size, especially little, tiny ones? They can fight back, but they're bound to lose in the end." He looked Dalton up and down. "You're a pretty big guy compared to her. She was what, four foot ten or eleven? Does that seem like a fair fight to you? Or are those the odds you like?"

Dalton shot to his feet, his hands balled into fists.

London backed off and Dalton realized he'd been baited. He'd given the detective what he wanted to see. He was too quick tempered. It was perhaps his worst failing, or at least that's what his father had told him on more than one occasion.

Dalton sat back down, running his hands through his hair. "Look, I'm sorry for that. I'm telling you, man to man, I would never hurt a woman."

"Bullshit! You don't fool me for a second with your expensive suit and Sunday manners. You'd hurt anyone who didn't give you what you wanted. Is that how it happened, McLagen? She was your brother's fiancé, but you wanted her, didn't you? Tried to force yourself on her and she let you have it?"

"No."

"You know, McLagen, you're a lawyer but maybe not a very good one because you wear your heart on your sleeve. You're very easy to read, so you must be a real hit in the courtroom. I'd say that's exactly what happened. You thought you'd try to take a little for yourself and she wasn't having it. She might not have been very big, but I'm guessing she was a feisty little thing."

"I didn't do what you're saying, nothing like it. You're wrong."

London watched him. "Look, I'm not saying you're a bad guy. A wise guy, yes, but you didn't deliberately set out to harm her, did you? Stuff happens. I understand that.

Things get out of hand. Tell me how it happened, Dalton. Tell me how the fight started between you and Sarah. Tell me how you panicked and saw your whole career floating away because of what you'd done. Tell me how you took her to that property where she was found. Did you know she liked roses? Is that why you buried her in a rose garden of all places? Was that the final kind thing you could do for her?"

"You're so far off base it's pathetic. I'm not answering any more of your questions."

London looked pointedly at the clock on the wall. "You know you're going to stay here until you do, don't you?"

"You have no right to keep me here. I haven't been charged with any crime."

"You're about to be. We'll see if your alibi checks out. And I hope you mentioned to this colleague of yours if he lies and gives you a phoney alibi, he's in a heap of trouble too. You did tell him that, didn't you, because if you didn't you've done him a disservice."

"My alibi will check out."

London shrugged indifferently. "Right now, it doesn't matter anyway because you still haven't told me who busted you in the mouth. Now, you take *that* along with those muddy shoes of yours and I have enough to charge you, my friend. Personally, I think you did this murder. I understand you might not be in a talkative frame of mind, so why don't you write it down nice and clear on paper for us? Make that confession like I'm guessing you're dying to. You see, maybe you didn't mean to kill her and maybe you did. I don't know, but that can't be changed. What can be changed is you acting like a man and owning up to it. That's what you can do for her now."

Dalton looked at the detective evenly. "You like to hear yourself talk, don't you? You like to put words in other peoples' mouths, but you won't put them in mine. Oh no you won't! I didn't kill Sarah Estey and that's a fact. I can certainly write *that* down for you if you like. As a matter of fact, if I write anything at all, that's what it'll be. I'm truly sorry someone did kill her though because she was a lovely young woman."

"And you were jealous of your brother. She liked him better than you, didn't she? If you couldn't have her no one could. Have I got that right?"

"No, you have not got that right. You think you have all the answers, but you don't."

"Okay then, suppose you tell me how it really was."

"This is a waste of time. I'm going to walk out of here as soon as your buddy gets back, because he can prove I'm telling you the truth. I saw from the newspaper story she was buried in a rose garden in Saint John. Where that was, I have no idea."

Just then the door opened and in walked Detective Halverson. "Cut him loose, Frank. His alibi checks out. As a matter of fact, he was at the guy's house on Tuesday night and at work all day."

Dalton stood, straightening his jacket unnecessarily. "Too bad you won't listen when someone is trying to tell you they're innocent, you might save yourselves a whole lot of time and trouble."

Halverson looked at Dalton without expression. "And the cow jumped over the moon. Get out of here and don't even think about leaving town. This is not over."

Dalton walked the few blocks back to his uptown office feeling like he'd survived a prizefight. Once back on the second floor of his building he walked through those doors like a man without a care in the world. He stopped at the typing pool where Nellie was talking to another secretary.

"Nellie," he said sharply. "Please bring your book and we'll finish that letter."

"Is everything all right, Mr. McLagen?" she asked as she hurried back to her own desk to retrieve her steno pad and pencil.

"Everything's fine!" he snapped. "Now come along with your book. This letter has to be out by the end of the day."

* * *

Maude tried to stay busy with cleaning chores to keep her mind off the funeral that was scheduled to take place the following day. She had no idea how she would ever get through that service. Never in a million years had she ever dreamed of a day like this, a funeral instead of a wedding. People had been very kind, the icebox overflowing with food delivered by caring members of the congregation and the community in general.

Cranston had been adamant he would perform the service although several people had tried to talk him out of it. He'd told her so. It never ceased to amaze her how he could remain so detached. It was as though he was talking about a stranger.

They were barely on speaking terms now, and that suited her fine. There wasn't much she wanted to say to him anyway, or him to her. If she had his meals on the table, he apparently saw no reason to engage her in conversation. The only time he was verbal at all was when he was grousing about something in the newspaper, and he had plenty to say about the media attention Sarah's murder was garnering.

Perhaps his grief was cloaked in anger. She hoped that was the explanation for his shocking indifference. Losing a son or a daughter was heart wrenching, a blow from which some people might never recover. Losing them in such a brutal way was unthinkable, yet Cranston soldiered on without emotion.

She herself was going through the motions as she cleared the dishes from the table, washed them and put them back in the cupboard. That wasn't much of a chore because there weren't many dishes to clean up. Her appetite had fled the moment she'd found Sarah's note and had never really returned. She felt hollow, and just when she thought she was drained of tears along came another deluge. She had to stay busy to keep her sanity.

She decided to tackle the back porch, something she'd planned to do two weeks ago as part of her spring cleaning. It seemed to be forever in need of straightening because Cranston was not a tidy person. Off came coats or hats, overshoes, whatever, and although there were places provided for everything, he never bothered to put anything where it belonged.

As she made her way to the back of the house her mind came to rest again on Sarah. She'd told the police she didn't want to know how her daughter had died, and until they caught the murderer they were understandably tight-lipped as to the cause of death anyway. The paper said they had Connor in custody, but it hadn't actually said he'd been charged with her murder. She thought again about that poor woman finding Sarah's body in her rose garden. Sarah had loved roses, so it had to be someone she knew who'd put her there. The story also said because of the rain and the heavy police presence the newly landscaped backyard was now a muddy mess. The whole thing was almost too much to bear, but at least tomorrow her daughter would finally be laid to rest in a proper Christian burial.

Once in the back porch she hung up Cranston's raincoat and set his umbrella aside to take to the stand out by the coat tree. There wasn't much tidying to do at all she realized, although the floor could do with a good scrubbing. She welcomed the chore if she could burn off some of this nervous energy. Before she set off for the scrub bucket and mop, she moved a box of books Cranston had put out here to take to the church for the rummage sale next month. It wasn't a big box, and she was able to shift it easily enough, but when she did, her heart gave a sickening lurch. Behind the box were Cranston's overshoes, and they were covered in dried mud.

Chapter Thirteen

Maude stared at the overshoes. Could it be? She snatched them up and marched to the study where Cranston was working on his remarks for Sarah's funeral service. Not bothering to knock as per his standing instructions, she strode into the room with muddy boots in hand.

He looked up from his notes as though she'd taken leave of her senses. "What ... what is going on?" he sputtered. "What are you bothering me about? Can't you see I'm working?"

She ignored him, holding up the boots. "I have a question for you, Cranston. What is the meaning of these boots being covered in mud?"

He gawked at her, nonplussed. "What is the meaning? The meaning is they're covered in mud and need to be cleaned. Why are you interrupting me to ask such a fool question? Why are you not cleaning them like you're supposed to be doing? It's a simple job."

"Why did you hide them?" she persisted. "I found them behind a box. I wouldn't have seen them if I hadn't moved those books you were supposed to take to the rummage sale. You weren't planning on me moving that box, were you!"

He was still looking at her, open-mouthed. "Hide them! I did not hide my boots. Why would I hide them? You're always carping at me about tracking up your porch floor, so I set them out of the way is all. Good grief!"

"I do not carp at you!"

"You most certainly do carp at me," he shouted. "Now go and clean those boots instead of standing there holding them like a ninny. I swear Maude, you're coming completely unhinged!"

She didn't move, her adrenalin still going full throttle. "No. I want you to tell me how you got mud on these overshoes, Cranston. There's no mud between the church and the parsonage. Certainly not enough to cause this kind of mess."

Cranston threw down his notes in disgust. "You infernal woman! I got the mud on my boots in the graveyard the other day. I could see from my window that Pensie Galbraith's grave was being dug in the wrong place, so I went out and spoke with Mansel Thorne the gravedigger before he got too far into his work. I had to go right up to him to be heard. As you also know the ground was saturated from that downpour the other night and I had my overshoes on. That's how they got muddy. There now, detective, are you satisfied?"

His explanation was completely plausible. She recalled they'd had the same problem with Mansel Thorne getting grave lots mixed up before. She was wrong but it would be a frosty day in hades before she apologized to him.

She turned to go.

"I asked you a question, Maude. What are you so worked up about? If I didn't know any better, I'd say you were about to make some very dangerous insinuations. You were, weren't you! Don't lose your nerve now. If you have something to say by all means say it and be done with it."

She turned back to face him. "All right then, Cranston. I've had my doubts from the beginning about whether you were involved in Sarah's disappearance. At first, I thought maybe you had sent her away. You were, are, so indifferent to her disappearance it's astonishing. It makes perfect sense that you somehow had a hand in her murder somewhere since you were so adamant about not involving the police or even bothering to find out where she was."

He gaped at her. "Are you saying I'm responsible for her death?"

Her courage was beginning to fray in the face of his glittering scrutiny. When he jumped to his feet, she cowered, yet managed to hold her ground. "As I said, I had my doubts. Anybody would have."

Cranston remained behind his desk, fuming. "Of all the despicable things to say!

You think I am no better than a murderer? Is that what you're trying to find it within yourself to tell me? This to a man who took in a whore's offspring and gave her a decent home? I stepped forward when no one else would and yet you dare to repay that generosity with an accusation of murder? It's probably the worst thing anyone has ever said to me. That is a vile insinuation, and from my own wife!"

She felt like wringing her hands but didn't. Cranston was frightening when he chose to be, but she didn't move a muscle. "I did not say you murdered her. What I am saying is you were involved somehow. You have been acting very mysterious. You did not appear at all anxious to find your own daughter. That's what makes me think you're involved."

"Involved how?" he roared.

"In burying her, all right? It said specifically in the newspaper the rose garden where they found Sarah was a muddy mess. When I saw your boots, what did you expect me to think after the way you've been acting?"

"You know, the whole business surrounding Sarah's murder has been rampant with speculation and you're about the only one who would believe everything that's been said. It's been a field day for the gullible and you were right in there with both feet, weren't you, Maude? And to think you'd take the word of some grandstanding reporter over your own husband. You ungrateful...."

But Maude was not to be subdued now that the floodgates had been thrown open. "Thomas Chaffee did it, didn't he? I've thought all along he had something to do with all of this. The way he looked at Sarah when they were at the table together that night. It was as though I saw Thomas for the first time when he was here last. He was absolutely leering at that poor girl. I could see as clear as day she was not only uninterested in marrying him, but he repulsed her. But you had it in your mind he was the man our daughter should marry and pushed relentlessly for it. You put his feelings ahead of hers. It was what *he* wanted, not her. I've since heard from Fanny that Thomas upset Sarah terribly. She was frightened of him."

He shook his head. "Frightened of him! Of all the preposterous things to say! It wasn't that long ago you were wanting the same thing, but you've changed your tune, haven't you?"

"Yes, I most certainly have. You had me buffaloed into thinking he would make the perfect husband for her, that she could join him in the mission field, and they would live happily ever after. I'm embarrassed and ashamed I was once in favour of an arranged marriage for Sarah. Everything is not always tied up in neat little package. You'd think I'd have learned my lesson long before now based on my own experience with an arranged marriage."

"I think you've gone completely off your rocker. You haven't taken to reading dime novels, have you? Thomas Chaffee helps people, Maude, he doesn't kill them."

"Are you sure about that? Why did he leave for Africa so quickly? He'd only just got home on furlough, saying how happy he was to be here and the next thing you know he's on his way back. I'm sure more people than me are wondering about that. Why did he suddenly feel the urge to return when he sat in this very house a few days ago and said how badly he needed a rest?"

Cranston spread his hands dramatically. "A man can't change his mind? He missed his work is all and so I did help him get back there as quickly as he could. Don't underestimate Thomas, he puts great store in being a missionary."

Maude squared her shoulders defiantly. "I don't believe you, Cranston. The whole thing sounds ... contrived, completely fabricated. I know he's a hard worker but him suddenly changing his mind like that doesn't make sense. I think Thomas is involved in Sarah's murder and I think you helped him cover it up. You were obsessed with having him marry Sarah. You are a man with a single purpose in life and that is to have your way no matter who it hurts or inconveniences," she threw at him recklessly.

"I'm not going to listen to any more of this hogwash. You're going off in all directions, as usual, and making no sense at all. You've become addlebrained with everything that's been happening. I'm going to call the doctor and have him come and give you a powder, otherwise you'll be making a fool of yourself at the funeral tomorrow. And put those confounded boots back in the porch where they belong before I whack you with one of them. That's what might be best for you anyway, to have some sense knocked into you."

She took a defensive step back, holding the boots out in front of her in the nature of a shield. "Don't you dare touch me, Cranston Estey. I have not taken leave of my senses, I'm coming *to* them and I'm not surprised you'd be intimidated by that. I think there's something going on all right between you and Thomas Chaffee, and until you tell me what it is I'll assume I'm right. Thomas Chaffee is the man they should be looking for, him and whoever helped him bury our poor daughter in that dreadful rose garden. You act suspicious, Cranston, and so therefore you'll be thought suspicious. It goes hand in glove as far as I'm concerned."

He glared at her ominously. "Don't be a fool, Maude. You're in way over your head."

"I could say the same about you."

"If you don't get out of this room right now with your bizarre accusations, I will make that call to the doctor. He'll understand. I'm sure it's not the first time he's had to deal with a hysterical female. Now leave and close the door behind you … and don't come back! Go lie down or whatever else would help. Do the right thing for once in your miserable life."

She knew when to leave although she was no less angry. "That's exactly what I'm going to do, the right thing. I'm going to call the police and tell them of my suspicions. Thomas has conveniently sailed away into the sunset hasn't he, but there are still ways to bring him back and account for his actions. You too."

He did come around the desk this time. "Do not make that telephone call, Maude Estey. You have no idea what you're dealing with and more to the point it's none of your business."

"My daughter's death is none of my business?"

Cranston was breathing heavily, his face scarlet. "Thomas Chaffee had nothing to do with Sarah's death. He would have made a wonderful husband for her. But no, instead, Sarah chose the son of one of this area's most corrupt men. Connor McLagen would have drawn her into that world, and it would have only been a matter of time before she was consumed by it. Go think about that in your obvious delirium because it wasn't all that long ago you agreed with me: *Cranston, we have to stop her from marrying into that family,* you told me. *Do something.* And yet

248

when I try to do something, push for Sarah to marry a strong, decent, God-fearing man, you side with our empty-headed daughter and reject him. You're as bad as she is. The both of you made a good pair."

"If Thomas had nothing to do with Sarah's murder, why all the subterfuge? Why was it necessary for him to flee the country at a moment's notice? Can't you see how that looks? Those are the actions of a guilty man, and you were part of it. I recall the state he was in when he came here Wednesday night. He looked distraught and then off the two of you went into the night. Was he upset because he missed The Belgian Congo? No, I hardly think so! It was something else, wasn't it? Something much worse."

"As usual you don't know what you're talking about."

She stood up to him, determined not to be run off. "Then tell me what's going on. I have a right to know. Something was up between the two of you. Was it a coincidence Sarah went missing during that time, and turned up murdered? I think not. Let's let the police decide what took place."

Cranston ran his hands through his hair in desperation, a glaring departure from a man who prided himself on always being in control. He dropped his hands to his side, returning to sit down heavily behind his desk.

"Maude, sit down," he said after a moment, pointing to the empty chair on her side of the desk. "You'll be the death of me, I have no doubt about that. It seems I have to take you into my confidence if I am to spare my good name any more public embarrassment. But you must swear not to repeat what I am about to tell you."

Her knees suddenly weak, she sank into the chair and dropped the boots onto the floor beside her. "I can't promise to do that, Cranston, if what you're about to tell me concerns the death of our daughter. Someone has to speak for *her*."

He leaned forward with his arms on the top of the desk, still in a position of power with hands folded and fingers steepled.

"It has nothing at all to do with Sarah, Maude, so get that out of your head. You need to calm yourself and stop running around making wild accusations. Everything is not what it seems, okay?"

"You mean with respect to Thomas' suspicious behaviour?"

"That's exactly what I mean. I don't think it should come as a shock to you when I say not only did Thomas think Sarah was the perfect choice of a wife for his work in The Belgian Congo, he was in love with her, deeply in love. Don't pretend you don't know Sarah had been promised to Thomas, but not because I was personally fond of the boy. It was because that's the direction I felt I was being led. I understood, until this whole thing blew up, you felt the same way. If Sarah wasn't so headstrong, she would be a married woman right now and on furlough with her husband."

"But that's not the way it went, is it, Cranston, because Sarah had her own mind, and I finally came to my senses. But all right, you have my word. I will not repeat what you are about to tell me to a living soul unless it involves the murder of our daughter. Then I most definitely will do what I have to do to find justice for her. I will no longer stay silent on her behalf. I want you to understand that before you say another word."

He nodded. "I understand, and this has absolutely nothing to do with Sarah, only in what affected Thomas took place the night of the dinner. It was her ultimate and I might add very rude rejection of him that drove him over the edge. If only she had been kinder, he would not have broken down the way he did. It was when he saw no possibility for them at all that he did something he shouldn't have done."

Maude felt ice water begin to flow through her veins. "What did he do?"

Cranston leaned back and folded his arms, quiet for a time as if choosing his next words carefully. "Thomas admits he was more distraught than he'd ever been in his life, completely devastated. When he chased after Sarah, he begged her to give him a chance and you know how that went. He felt she made a fool of him, and he was right. He was very angry. Unfortunately, instead of coming back here and talking to me, he returned to where he was staying as a guest for a few days. As you know, Allistair McPhee has been a deacon in our church for many years and he and Thomas had become quite friendly.

"Gertrude, his daughter, never married and since her mother died has kept house for her father. Thomas managed to keep his bitter disappointment of Sarah's rejection in check, but it continued to fester inside him. Then on Wednesday evening when Allistair was not at home, he reached his boiling point. Everyone, including Thomas knew that Gertrude had always carried a torch for him. In any event Gertrude was acting flirtatious and Thomas lost his head with the state of mind he was in. He forced himself on Gertrude I'm sorry to say. I apologize for speaking about such an indelicate matter, but you wanted the truth and there it is, the unvarnished version. Thomas says that later he was in such a state he didn't know what else to do but come to see me. I drove him to his mother's home in Saint John. He told me Gertrude had threatened to set the police on him for what he'd done, and he was beside himself. He was out of his mind. He even threatened to jump from the Reversing Falls Bridge. I tell you he was nearly catatonic.

"I finally managed to quiet him after some hours. I also had his hysterical mother to deal with. She begged me to save her son any way I could so he wouldn't have to go to prison for the rest of his life if he was convicted. He might even be put to death, and for certain he would be flogged. I promised I would book passage the following day on the next ship that could take him there and luckily there was one leaving Friday morning. I also arranged to cancel his furlough and have him sent back to Africa. On my way back from Saint John, I stopped at Allistair's home and spoke with him. We decided between the two of us it would be best if Thomas remained in Africa indefinitely. He understood Thomas' emotions had gotten the better of him and he wasn't himself when the act took place, that Gertrude had incited him."

Maude was outraged. "And Gertrude? What about her?"

"Her father managed to convince her it would be best to drop the whole matter, that she would be publicly humiliated should such a thing be paraded before the courts. It might not even get that far if Thomas were to say it was consensual. That she had led him on because everyone knew she was besotted with him. It was in her best interests to put it all behind her, forget it ever happened and move on."

"Poor Gertrude, like she could ever forget such a terrible experience."

"Poor *Gertrude!* Poor Thomas, although I do agree it was an unfortunate incident...."

"Is that what rape is, an unfortunate incident?"

"In this case, yes. So as I was saying, why ruin a man's impeccable reputation because of one unfortunate incident? Besides, if it helps any, he's been sick about it since it happened. He's having trouble living with himself."

"I should think so! And to think he was the man we chose for our daughter. If he had no better control of himself than that, what kind of a life would Sarah have had?"

"A very good one, I expect, as long as she behaved herself. So you see, Maude, there's nothing nefarious going on here. Thomas did not murder Sarah and I did not help him bury her body. It was all perfectly innocent and easily explained."

"Perfectly innocent," she repeated absently. "And may I ask what you mean when you say *behave herself*?"

Cranston sighed, already tired of the conversation. "A woman should know her place is what I'm saying. That's something you should have taught Sarah. She could have done well with such lessons because it was her impudence that drove Thomas to do what he did."

Maude studied her husband of thirty-seven years, his hawkish nose, impossibly high forehead and angry slash of a mouth. How could she have ever thought him handsome? Sitting before him now, she did not find him even remotely attractive. She wondered, as she'd often done, what it would be like to love the man you slept next to every night? To feel passion? Was that what it was like for Sarah and Connor? He was a handsome devil to be sure. It was as if lights were now being turned on inside her, new light shining into old corners that had only known darkness, until now. At fifty-three she did not feel at all like *behaving* anymore to avoid her husband's wrath, or for any other reason.

Her gaze shifted to the muddy boots sitting on the floor by her chair. She would no doubt be scolded for any dirt that had shaken free onto the carpet because Cranston insisted on a spotless home. It was as if suddenly those boots had become the metaphor for what was wrong with their marriage, had always been wrong with it. Her job would always be to clean his boots.

"Cranston," she said at last, "tomorrow we will bury our daughter, the only child we'll ever have."

He listened, clearly annoyed as he waited for her to go on.

"And when that dreadful task is finished and we are left with the rest of our lives to get on with, we will not be getting on with them together. You told me to leave this house when this was over, and I'll be doing just that. Leaving you."

He threw back his head in exasperation then slammed the palms of his hands onto the desk. "Maude, what are you going on about? What's the matter *now*?"

Her eyes caught his and held. "I'm saying I no longer wish to be Mrs. Cranston Estey. That's what I'm going on about. I want us to go our separate ways."

He shook his head with purpose. "That is never going to happen so forget about it. I spoke in anger previously because you drove me to it. What do you expect, always harping at me. But you are to stay right where you are because the scandal would be too great if you left. I have my reputation to consider, and I will not allow you to tarnish it with your featherbrained ways. You are my wife, and you will stay by my side where you belong."

"Your reputation be damned! I don't love you, Cranston. I never have. Living with you is intolerable."

He stared at her incredulously. "What's love got to do with any of this? A reverend needs a wife and that is what you were chosen to take on. You willingly married me and it's a role for life, Maude, or weren't you paying attention? Marriage is not something you can opt out of whenever you choose. You as the reverend's wife have an important part to play. If you were to leave me, think about the message that would send to the congregation, to young couples considering marriage. What about the Woman's Missionary Society you lead? You have Sunday school students who look up to you. If only any of those people could hear the terrible things you say to me, the burden *I* have to bear with you for a wife. It's for the sake of decency that I do."

"Do you love me, Cranston?"

"No, I do not! The only woman I ever loved was no good. Much too young, she...."

The light, as it continued to illuminate dark spaces, was blinding. "Cranston! That wayward young woman in our church, Winifred Collicut! She.... You are Sarah's natural father, aren't you?"

"Are you really that dimwitted you haven't been able to figure that out before now? Of course I'm Sarah's natural father, but my seed was wasted on that little tramp. She was sent to test me, and I failed, don't you see? And I have paid for that one mistake for eighteen years."

Maude was reeling. "*You* paid! *She* paid because you never once showed her an ounce of love."

"Because she was too much like her mother! I could see it from the start! She was impossible, just like her mother, Winifred. No good! Now go off and do whatever it is you do and leave me to my work. Go! And there'll be no more talk about leaving. I forbid it!"

Maude got shakily to her feet. She had to get out of this room before she exploded from natural combustion. She bent and picked up the boots, priding herself that she resisted the urge to hurl them at him.

She closed the door quietly behind her just as she had done all these many years, because a mouse must always try to slip away undetected. It tries to keep out of everyone's way, remain silent. But she did throw the boots when she got to the back porch, and they crashed against the far wall just missing the window. If Cranston was curious about the noise, he never bothered to investigate.

There were no tears as she went into Sarah's room. Surprisingly it still looked the same despite the seismic shift in her own life since Sarah had last lived there. The hours between now and the funeral stretched before her like a long dark tunnel, and she knew the best thing was to try to stay busy or else she would go out of her mind.

She picked up the wedding dress again, a stunning creation her daughter would have worn to perfection.

The police already had what they were looking for from the room, so taking matters into her own hands she laid the dress aside then tackled Sarah's bureau, cleaning out each drawer. After the funeral was over tomorrow, she'd pack what there was for storage. There was very little jewellery to go through, but she came across the gold pendant she and Cranston had given their daughter when she'd graduated high school, and a silver bracelet when she'd earned her teaching license. Sarah was a smart girl, a modern woman who knew what she wanted.

She thought of Sarah's last moments, something never far from her mind. She wasn't able to parcel everything away like

Cranston could. She wondered, had death come quickly or had she suffered? She balled her fists and pressed them to her eyes at the notion of suffering. And by whose hand had she died? Was it indeed Connor? No! She couldn't believe that, but the police were no closer to solving the crime now than they had been two days ago. Then again it was still early as these things went. The thought that the murder could remain unsolved was too unsettling to think about.

Next she went to the small desk in the corner where Sarah prepared her lessons. Cranston had found it in the basement of the church many years ago and lugged it home for her to use. Maude had thought that very kind of him. She remembered how pleased Sarah had been when she'd seen it, flying across the room to hug him. She also recalled Cranston had not hugged her back.

Focusing again, she found a hand-covered lesson book, a stack of lined paper, a box of pencils and the ever-popular ballpoint pens. Sarah loved them and had several bound with an elastic band in the top drawer. But nowhere in any of the three drawers did she find the type of paper Sarah had used for her note, and there was certainly no sign of a fountain pen. Another lightning bolt struck. Sarah had not written the note at all! She was sure the police already knew because it appeared as if the desk had been searched. It'd been convenient that the window was usually left open. The note must have been placed on the table from outside the building. Her daughter was likely already dead when she'd found the note, and she swallowed bile. The killer had been right outside their home while they slept.

* * *

The front desk sergeant looked up as an unkempt thirtyish-looking man of medium height and weight approached him without hesitation. There was an air of expectancy about him.

"Can I help you?" the sleepy-eyed officer asked, his twelve-hour shift just about at an end.

"Yes, you can," the man said as he stared straight ahead, unblinking. "I can't live with myself any longer. I am here to confess to the murder of that schoolteacher. I'm the one who killed her."

Chapter Fourteen

The desk sergeant snapped to attention. "I beg your pardon?"

"I said I have to confess to the murder of that woman, the one who was buried in a garden. I have to do the right thing, whatever happens to me."

The man was quickly ushered inside and seated before being joined by additional police personnel. "Tell us all about it," said the officer sitting across from him, pencil poised over paper, "starting with how you killed her."

"I stabbed her over and over. There was blood everywhere."

The officer sighed loudly as he exchanged meaningful glances with the other officers before settling back in his chair, eyeing the self-proclaimed suspect. "Are you sure about that?"

The man's beetle brows knit together giving him the appearance of someone much older. "Isn't that how she died?"

The officer laid down the pencil. "Get out of here."

"Don't you want to know who did it? I'm confessing!"

"To a crime you didn't commit you mean. Go on, go home and let us get on with our work."

The man was crestfallen. "She wasn't stabbed? Was she strangled? I did it I tell you!"

The officer sat back in his chair, weary. "I said get out of here, or I'll have you charged with mischief."

The man, red-faced, did as he was told and headed for the door with great haste.

Most sensational stories, and thank heaven they didn't come around very often, brought out the attention seekers. Everyone wanted to be in the limelight, some worse than others. Apparently anyone who would confess to a murder they didn't commit was delusional, but it happened.

* * *

People came from far and wide for Sarah's funeral, many on foot from surrounding areas. The road and churchyard were packed with automobiles carrying loved ones, friends and colleagues, and not surprisingly, the curious. The police were even in attendance although they kept a very low profile.

Connor, looking much the worse for wear fell into line with the mourners filing solemnly into the sanctuary.

Cranston, who was standing close by, spied him and sprang into action. "Do not set a foot in this church, McLagen," he warned as he intercepted Sarah's ex-fiancé. "We do not want you here. You are not welcome."

Connor stopped. "I want to attend Sarah's funeral. I have a right to be here. She was going to be my wife. I loved her! Please!"

Cranston was adamant. "I told you to leave and if you don't go quietly, I will have you thrown out. I can't imagine why you're not still in custody anyway. You obviously lied in order to get released because there's no doubt in my mind it was you who murdered my daughter. Now leave these premises at once or I'll take you in hand myself!"

Connor hesitated, people had begun to stare at him and sidle away as though they'd be guilty by association if they dared get too close.

Fire was flying from Cranston's eyes. "I said leave! Let us alone to grieve for Sarah, to mourn her properly without her murderer looking on with alligator tears."

Connor felt sick at heart as he recognized Saint John Police detectives London and Halverson quickly moving up beside him. "You've been asked to leave, Mr. McLagen," said London quietly, "so I would strongly suggest you do just that. Now."

Connor gritted his teeth. "I want to be here. She was my fiancé and I should not be prevented from attending her funeral. What's being done to me is inhuman."

London moved closer. "You heard her father. You're not wanted here. Now leave quietly or we will escort you to your car and see you off this property ourselves."

Connor stepped out of the queue headed into the church, his anger quickly coming to a boil. "This is a public place!" he said through his teeth. "You cannot stop me from attending this service!"

London took hold of his arm, a vicelike grip that Connor remembered all too well. "Listen up. This is *not* a public place. You are trespassing on private property, and you've been asked to leave. Now, do you want to be arrested here in front of all these people? If not, I would suggest you turn on that expensive heel of yours and backtrack out of here. Pronto."

Shaking with anger Connor did as he was told. He had done nothing wrong, nothing to hurt Sarah or her family but to many people he was still a suspect. He knew it gave her father great pleasure to have him thrown out and he had no choice but to go. In his haste to exit the churchyard he came close to striking another vehicle. Extricating himself from that near collision he drove to the Point, parked out of sight by some trees near the ferry landing, and wept.

* * *

The service was understandably lengthy in salute to a young woman who had died so tragically. Fanny had asked permission to deliver a brief eulogy and Cranston had reluctantly accommodated her. By the time she got to the pulpit she was in such a state it didn't appear as though she would be able to get through it. She paused a moment to collect herself as Cranston had suggested she do if she felt overcome, and after a few deep breaths began her tribute.

"Sarah Estey was my best friend," she began, her voice still wobbly. "We were more like sisters I guess because neither one of us had one. We first met when we were ten years old, and I came to live not far from her. We became immediate friends. We were always up to some sort of hijinks together, and what fun we had. We were rarely apart.

"Sarah and I made a pact and I know this sounds strange because we were just children when we did it, but we decided whichever one of us got married first, the other had to be the maid of honour. The first one of us to have a child, we would name it after the other...." She broke down again and it was a minute or two before she regained her composure. "And the first one to die, the other would deliver the eulogy." Fanny paused to mop her eyes.

"She loved life, every minute of it and it doesn't seem real she's actually gone. I still can't believe it and I miss her dreadfully. I feel guilty I'm the one who was left behind and there have been days since this whole thing happened that I wished I was with her now."

There was a murmuring throughout the crowd. Some could be heard openly weeping, Maude Estey sobbing into a handkerchief in the front row.

"Sarah was an outstanding teacher, everyone said so, and that was something else we shared. She was at a happy place in her life, about to be married...." And at this point she broke down completely and could not go on. Cranston ushered her down the steps to her seat beside Maude who reached and took her hand.

Once back behind the pulpit Cranston continued, remembering the all-too-brief life of his daughter. Maude wondered why he couldn't have showed that kindness when Sarah was still alive. Following the service mourners made the short trek to the cemetery where the committal service was conducted. And then it was done. Sarah had finally been laid to rest.

As had been announced by Cranston at the conclusion of the service, a reception was being held in the basement of the church and that's where the subdued throng was now headed.

Fanny was standing on the periphery of the crowd when she noticed two men approaching her. "I'm Detective Frank London from the Saint John Police Department," the taller man said, offering his hand, "and this is my partner, Detective

Peter Halverson. First of all, let me speak for both of us when I say how sorry we are for your loss. It must be very difficult. I understand you're a teacher too, so with school out for the summer I'll bet you're planning to get away from everything for a while; help put this tragedy out of your mind."

Fanny nodded, crying. "That's exactly what I'm planning as soon as I get home from here," she managed. "I'm going to stay with friends in Nova Scotia. I may even move there, I'm not quite sure yet what I'm going to do."

Halverson spoke softly. "I wonder if we could speak with you for a few moments since we're already all the way out here. I hope you don't mind. I'm sure you're as anxious to help solve this case for your friend as we are."

Fanny was still trying to stem her flow of tears, without result. "I'll be happy to speak with you if it will help, but first let me tell my aunt and uncle I won't be going back home with them. They're not staying for the reception. I'll be right back." True to her word she re-joined the detectives moments later. "Maybe we could talk over in the parsonage instead of standing here in the yard," she suggested. "I see Mrs. Estey talking to Marion Bimble. Let me ask her if she minds us using her living room for a few minutes. I'm sure it'll be fine."

Maude had no objection, so within minutes the three were seated in the Estey living room. Fanny was edge of seat in an armchair, the detectives claiming the sofa.

Fanny turned to London who seemed to be the friendlier of the two. "I'm wondering how close you are to finding Sarah's killer? As I said, I will do anything I can to help."

London watched her. "Well now, Fanny, we're very glad to hear that's how you feel. An investigation is all about knitting pieces together, nothing is too insignificant to tell us about. And sometimes people get small details wrong. They're mistaken in what they can recollect. Remember that?"

She nodded, colouring slightly. "I know you're talking about me, but I usually have an excellent memory. A real mind for detail, which as you can imagine comes in handy as a schoolteacher. I teach grades three and four and that keeps me on my toes. But I can see what you mean, because I did think I saw Connor's car and you say it wasn't him at all. Did you ever find out who it was?"

Halverson leaned toward Sarah. "That's precisely what you can help us clear up because there seems to be a discrepancy. You see, Sarah's mother told the police that on the night her daughter died you and she had been into the city running some last-minute errands before the wedding."

Fanny looked at both detectives, her brow knit. "Yes, but we went all over this when we talked before. I don't think I have anything new to add."

London adjusted his position on the sofa. "That's right, we have talked before but sometimes a person's memory is jogged, and they think of something else. We're hoping this will be the case today. You say you don't mind talking to us again and we appreciate that. You say you went into Saint John."

Fanny nodded again, fighting back a fresh wave of tears. "That is correct," she said at length. "We had to pick up her shoes at the Manchester, Robertson & Allison department store on King Street, and a few other items for her trousseau."

London waited for her to continue, Halverson ready to note any new information. "And then you started back home," London prompted.

She glanced at him. "That's right, but first we had scones with strawberries in MRA's tearoom. We both loved those. They were our one guilty pleasure. It didn't take us long though, I'd say about an extra half hour."

London crossed one long leg over the other. "And you were driving your uncle's vehicle?"

"Yes. He uses it as part of his job with the Dunphy estate. It was my uncle who taught me how to drive. It was a real treat for Sarah and me to be allowed to use it. We were very excited. We hurried to finish her errands, so we'd have some time for ourselves and still be home before dark."

London led her along gently. "Sounds like a lot of fun, and you made it back home in time?"

Fanny thought for a moment. "It was only a little after seven o'clock, so Sarah had decided to walk to her house because it was such a lovely night and then Connor ... I mean...."

London pursed his lips as he listened. "Oh right, the car that came along just at that time."

Fanny dried her eyes again. "You know I do wonder who that was."

London folded his arms, never taking his eyes off her. "So do we."

Fanny nodded absently.

Halverson sighed. "Tell us about that again, Fanny, if you don't mind."

Fanny sniffed, recounting how a black Model T had stopped at her home and how Sarah had gone off with whomever was driving it. She also added that she'd heard an argument as they drove away. Both London and Halverson listened patiently as she recounted her version of events.

When she finished, London was still studying the floor before once again meeting her eyes. "Do you think whoever was in that car had been waiting for her? Following you out the road from Saint John? Because whoever it was seemed to get there just as you arrived."

Fanny shrugged. "I don't think we were being followed. They were simply coming along at the same time. Maybe it was someone keeping tabs on her, you never know. That's why I automatically assumed it was Connor. That's something he'd do."

It was a moment before London spoke. "Again, we're just trying to keep everything straight because we asked Connor about doing that, coming along and picking Sarah up after you came back from the city on Tuesday night. Remember?"

Fanny's hanky was obviously too damp to be of any real value, yet she still pressed it into use. "It was definitely Tuesday night because we taught that day and handed out the report cards. I never forget a date. I do recall Detective Halverson calling me to go over that again. I said I couldn't swear it was Connor McLagen's car I saw, but the more I think about it I believe I *could* swear it was him. I remember it very clearly."

London nodded again. "It seems that Connor does too, as does his father and his father's secretary. Connor was at his office working late on Tuesday night and so was his father and Mrs. Daniels, McLagen senior's secretary. She was able to verify his statement, and so you see, Connor McLagen's alibi for Tuesday night is what we call airtight. I'm sure you'll agree he couldn't be in two places at once, especially with those two places being so far apart. Like you say, you wonder who that was. No ideas at all?"

Fanny could feel her face catch fire. "I have no idea, but I've been thinking. Maybe Connor is lying. He probably paid his father's secretary to lie for him. They have enough money to do something like that. It's possible."

London didn't take his eyes off her. "Other people saw him there too, apparently quite a few. There's no mistake about it, he was not in your yard on Tuesday night. He was in his office in downtown Saint John. That leaves us with a mystery man...."

Fanny had begun to fidget. "Whoever it was he was very angry. It was probably right after I saw him that he killed her because they were shouting. I heard him threaten her life! I did!"

Halverson cocked his head sideways. "Oh? You must have forgotten to mention that to us earlier, because it's the first we've heard of it."

Her eyes darted from one detective to the other. "Well, he did. As a matter of fact, I knew in my heart I would never see her alive again."

London stared at her. "You actually heard that? Can you recall the exact words?"

Fanny was silent for a moment. "It was very clear. He said I'm going to kill you."

Halverson was busy making notes, he and London exchanging a brief glance before London spoke. "Why didn't you call the police and report such a thing? A death threat is a criminal offence, not to mention your friend was in danger."

Fanny hesitated. "Well...."

London tried again. "Fanny, you just told us you heard someone threaten the life of your best friend."

She dissolved into tears again. "I'm so confused. All of this has been like a nightmare."

London unfolded his arms and bent forward, elbows on knees. "Fanny, why don't you tell us what really happened that night, I mean between you and Sarah? Did you have an argument?"

Fanny began to cry harder. "Argument? No, we didn't have an argument. There was nothing to argue about. She was getting ready to marry one of the most eligible bachelors around. Her life was perfect, just like a fairy tale."

London nodded his head knowingly. "And you were jealous?"

Fanny shook her head. "No, hardly. I adored Sarah. I tell you she went off in that car...

London studied her at length. "Come on, Fanny. There was no car, was there? That makes you the last person to see Sarah alive."

Fanny continued to sob, the shake of her head barely perceptible.

Halverson puffed a sigh. "Fanny, tell us about the note you left in Sarah's room. You wrote it, didn't you? We knew as soon as we searched her room she hadn't written it. There was no plain white paper in her desk, no fountain pen, no bottle of ink. But I'll bet you've got all of those things at home if we were to take a look, don't you?"

She could barely speak for sobbing but managed to nod her head. "Yes, I wrote the note. God help me, I did. I didn't know what else to do. I was so scared. My handwriting is very similar to Sarah's, and I hoped her mother wouldn't be able to tell the difference. I think of the people I've deceived, hurt. I think of never seeing Sarah again. That will be my punishment for the rest of my life. Nothing anyone did would ever be worse than that."

She wept bitterly.

London reached ahead and laid his hand on her arm, and she looked up. "Tell us what happened, Fanny. How did you kill her?"

More tears came as she hiccupped on sobs. "It was the blow to the head that killed her."

Halverson and London both nodded their heads knowingly. The cause of death had not been released because of the ongoing investigation. Only the police knew the autopsy had determined the cause of death to be blunt force trauma to the head.

"We know,'" said Halverson.

Fanny bent double. "Oh, I am a horrible person," she wailed, her head wrapped in her arms.

Tapping her on the shoulder, London passed her a fresh white handkerchief from the breast pocket of his jacket. "Try to calm yourself if you can and tell us everything. You're going to have to talk about it sooner or later and this is better than doing it at the police station. Come on," he encouraged her, "take a deep breath and get it over with. You'll feel better when you do."

Fanny took the handkerchief and murmured her thanks before wiping her eyes. "I loved Sarah. She was the best friend I'll ever have in this life. There will never be anyone like her again. She was so kind, so full of life. We had such good times together. I guess you could say we were both daredevils, egging the other one on to do the ... forbidden. We were always up to something. We had a lot of fun together."

She continued without being prompted. "I loved her and now she's gone, and I'm horrified by the whole thing. Horrified! I've hardly been able to sleep or eat since it happened. You're right, Detective London, I'm actually glad to talk about it and I should have gone to you long before now because I hated the pretence, the lies I had to tell. What will they do to me?"

Halverson huffed a pent-up sigh. "That's for a judge to decide, not us. Now, Fanny, you're leaving out a lot of details. We know this is not easy, but please tell us exactly what happened and where it happened. Take your time and tell us the whole story, everything. Take another deep breath and try to collect yourself."

Halverson flipped another page in his small notebook and wet the pencil with the tip of his tongue in readiness.

Fanny was silent for a moment. "There was some blood although I guess most of the bleeding happened on the inside. I tried to talk to her, tell her I was sorry, but I could tell right away she was dead. I don't think she suffered."

When Fanny lapsed into silence again, London urged her to continue. "Fanny, why don't you start at the beginning? That's always the best way to go about it. Okay?"

"All right," she whispered, her voice wavering. "I'll go back to the beginning, but this is terribly hard to talk about." She took a deep breath, expelling it tremulously. "I think I already told you that after Sarah finished her errands, we had scones in MRA's tearoom and we enjoyed them so much. When we came out of the store we were in high spirits. It was such a beautiful night. I mean, there'd been a shower earlier, but the sun was out again and it was really nice. Neither one of us wanted to go home right away even though I'd promised my uncle I'd return early.

"We drove up to Lily Lake and sat by the water for a while, walked around and looked at the gardens. We both like flowers and Sarah was telling me how she planned to have a rose garden at her new house, the one

Connor built for them to move into when they returned from their honeymoon. She was going to ask him about having a rose garden because they were her favourite flower. It was then that I remembered hearing my uncle telling my aunt about the rose garden a friend of his, a gardener, was helping to install at a new mansion on the east side of Saint John. Uncle Frederick said Bill, that was the gardener's name, was sick at the moment and things were held up a bit, but he'd probably finish planting in the new week. Apparently Bill had told him it was one of the biggest rose gardens he'd ever seen on a private estate, a real show place. My aunt didn't know exactly where my uncle was talking about, so he'd described where it was located.

"Anyway, I suggested to Sarah that we go there and have a look around. It'd be fun. Uncle Frederick said the mansion itself had just been finished but the family hadn't moved in yet, so what would it hurt? Sarah could see the rose garden and get an idea as to how she wanted hers to look, and we'd have one more lark before she got married and settled down. She was all for it so off we went.

"I found the mansion with no trouble but when we went up the driveway there was this tall wrought-iron fence around the property and big gates with a sign that said PRIVATE, NO TRESSPASSING. VIOLATORS WILL BE PROSECUTED. I was going to turn around and leave. You couldn't see the rose garden from where we were anyway, but Sarah said wouldn't it be daring to climb the fence and go take a real quick look. So we did it and managed to climb that fence even though we were wearing dresses.

"The garden was spectacular. Sarah loved it. We were almost finished looking around when we thought we heard a vehicle coming so we started running as fast as we could back along one of the garden paths headed for the entrance. We knew we'd be in big trouble if we got caught. That's when Sarah caught her toe on one of the cobblestones and was pitched forward. She struck her head hard on the edge of the stone sundial. It made a loud cracking sound, like bone was breaking. It was sickening. She then fell sort of sideways. She landed face up in the long trench dug to plant the rest of the rosebushes standing nearby waiting to be set into the ground. The hole in the rose bed was maybe two or three feet wide and deep enough to plant those great big rosebushes.

"I crawled into the hole and tried to revive her, thinking maybe she was just knocked out but like I said earlier, I could tell she was already dead. There was no pulse, and her eyes were open. She wasn't breathing. I didn't know what to do. I knew I couldn't carry her up over the fence on my own to take her out because I wasn't strong enough, and the gates were locked. What could I have done?"

London was listening intently. "You said you heard a vehicle. Couldn't you have gotten help from them? Try to find a neighbour?"

Fanny shook her head, tears still falling. "I ran to the entrance but there was no vehicle. The road went past the estate so whoever it was must have kept on going. But it was already too late. I ran back to Sarah. I have never been in such a state in my life. I knew we had been trespassing and I didn't want anyone to find me there. I didn't want my uncle and aunt to find out I'd broken the law and might be sent to jail. They'd be so ashamed of me, maybe even ask me to leave their home. And I was fearful of losing my teaching position if I was prosecuted. I'd never get another position anywhere if I had a police record, so my career would be over. I knew Sarah was already dead, so I started covering her over. I kept saying I'm sorry, I'm sorry the whole time. Then I tried to plant the rosebushes over her, but they wouldn't stand up right because there wasn't enough room. I kept scooping soil from the pile beside the hole to help pack them in place. I was so terrified someone would come before I got out of there. I buried her as best I could then ran back to the entrance, climbed over the fence and drove home. I was so frantic I barely remember the drive."

London's eyebrows hiked. "You did all that so you wouldn't lose your job? Have your aunt and uncle mad at you?"

Fanny hung her head. "I'm sorry. I didn't know what else to do."

The look that passed between London and Halverson spoke volumes as Fanny went on with her story. "My dress, socks and shoes were a mess from digging in the soil, but my uncle and aunt were still with their friends next door when I got home. I changed and washed my clothes by hand and hung them on the line. Then I wrote the note that was supposedly from Sarah. I had to rewrite it at least a dozen times because my hands were shaking so bad. I burned the failed attempts in the kitchen stove the next day.

"By the time my uncle and aunt returned home I was already in bed, so I didn't have to talk to them. I waited until they were asleep to take the note down to the parsonage. I knew the layout of the room because I'd gone there with Sarah from time to time. I remembered she liked to leave her window open for fresh air. That part was easy. I opened the screen panel, put the note on the table and set the MRA bags with the shoes and stuff on the floor beside the table. It was awful creeping around like that in the dark. I was terrified someone would see me but fortunately no one did. I was still shaking when I got back home and managed to get to my room without being heard."

She dropped her head into her hands again on an anguished wail and it was a minute or two before she could continue. "The next day I tried to act as normal as I could, but it was hard to lie to Mrs. Estey when she came to the school looking for Sarah." She looked up at the two detectives, meeting their eyes full on for the first time. "You must think I'm some kind of monster. That's how I think of myself. I never thought I was capable of any of this, but...."

Halverson ran his hand over his face. "You're not a monster, Fanny. You panicked. People lose their minds and do things they wouldn't ordinarily ever think of doing when they're in a state of panic, and it sounds like that's what happened here. But I have to tell you, you made some very bad decisions for someone your age ... a schoolteacher."

Fanny's tears ran freely. "I admit that, but you have to believe Sarah's death was an accident. I wouldn't lie to you about that."

London adjusted his position on the sofa. "Even though you've been lying to us all along. That's the problem with lying, Fanny. When you do finally get around to the truth, we think maybe it's just another lie."

Fanny's eyes widened. "I know I lied before but this is the truth, I swear. I did not kill Sarah, she tripped and fell while we were running. It was a terrible accident." She hung her head. "And I'm so sorry I tried to blame poor Connor. He didn't deserve any of this because he had nothing to do with it at all. I know he loved her, and I took her away from him. I'm ashamed of myself that I did what I did, but I just couldn't think straight at the time."

Halverson glanced at Fanny's bare fingers. "But you knew enough to remove her engagement ring, didn't you?"

"Yes," she admitted. "It didn't seem right that something so valuable shouldn't be put away in a safe place. It's in my jewellery box at home."

At this she broke down again and it was a few minutes before she could go on. When it seemed she had recovered enough, London pressed ahead. "What were you planning to do with the ring? Sell it?"

She was indignant. "Certainly not! I was thinking about mailing it to Connor anonymously, I don't know."

London looked at her evenly. "It's still at your home? In your jewellery box you say?"

"Yes," she said not looking at either man. "It's there."

London rolled his shoulders, his back likely aching from the stiff horsehair chesterfield. "So if we went there right now you could show us the ring."

Fanny hesitated. "Yes. What do you plan to do with it?"

Halverson looked surprised. "Give it back to Sarah's fiancé. I wouldn't suggest you take it to him. He might not be all that interested in talking to you considering everything you've told us. In any event you do have to come back to Saint John with us because we will be charging you. We'll stop and get the ring on the way so it can be returned to Connor McLagen."

Fanny's head flew up, her eyes wide with fright. "Charge me with murder you mean? I didn't kill her, I just buried Sarah."

Halverson's face was set. "Charges relating to that, yes. Like I said it will be up to a judge to decide what happens to you in this case. Even if, as you say, Sarah's death was an accident, it's what you did with her body after that. You lied to police and interfered with our investigation. Those are all criminal acts, Fanny, and you'll have to answer for them. If you're ready, we'll leave now. Please get hold of yourself and get to your feet."

She could not be comforted. "I am the most horrible person in the world!" She sobbed uncontrollably. "I did a horrible thing! I do want you to take me away from here, and I don't ever want to look back."

Epilogue

Fanny Hobson pleaded guilty to charges relating to the improper burial of a dead body as well as obstruction of justice. Her lawyer pleaded for leniency considering the circumstances, but his young client still faced incarceration.

One week after the funeral, Maude Estey moved out of the parsonage and accepted the position of live-in housekeeper at the home of busy dressmaker, Mabel Walker.

Connor married Gladys Biddington in the fall of 1928 and went on to father six healthy McLagen sons.

Thomas Chaffee died of severe dengue fever in 1929 in The Belgian Congo. He was laid to rest there in a small village graveyard.

Fanny married Herbert Deerfield, a farmer from nearby Meehan's Cove in 1930. The couple raised eight children.

The church hired a housekeeper for the parsonage, and life continued uninterrupted for Reverend Cranston Estey until his death in 1932 from a massive stroke.

McLagen & Son Ltd. weathered Prohibition in fine style, not only emerging unscathed from that political debacle, but with greatly improved profits.

Pritchard and Agnes McLagen continued to enjoy life on Orchard Hill, turning in the proper social circles. Proud grandparents, they adored their six boisterous grandsons.

Dalton McLagen was spotted on more than one occasion placing flowers on Sarah's grave. He never married.

The End

If you enoyed this book, please leave a review. Thank you!

Eden Monroe books published by BWL Publishing

Barlowe Pride
Sudden Turn
Looking for Snowflakes
Sidelined
Dangerous Getaway
Almost Broken
Just Before Sunset
Unforeseen Shadows
Incomplete Truths
Storms in the Valley
Back in the Valley
When Fate Comes Calling
Gold Digger Among Us
Dare to Inherit

BWL Author
Eden Monroe

Eden Monroe loves giving voice to the endless parade of interesting characters that introduce themselves in her imagination. She writes about real life, real issues and struggles, and triumphing against all odds. A proud east coast Canadian, she enjoys a variety of outdoor activities, her cat, and a good book.

BWL Publishing

BWL

bwlpublishing.ca